Terramare 3: what a planet to be stuck on. Flatter than a pan-cake, colder than a deep-freeze, featureless as a billiard ball, and teeming with poisonous gases. And Noll's and Niven's jobs aren't much better either. They are both Cargostrippers Grade 1 and spend their days loading and unloading freight.

The only thing that makes life bearable is the two boys' secret hobby – Wheelie, a superb motorbike they'd discovered on Earth, smuggled to Terramare bit by bit and gradually put together again. Not that there is much chance they'll ever be able to ride her for how are they to get hold of any petrol?

Solving this problem is only the start of Nicholas Fisk's exciting adventure story which culminates in a nerve racking climax. Both entertaining and chilling, *Wheelie in the Stars* will be enjoyed by readers of eleven and over.

Nicholas Fisk

Wheelie in the Stars

Puffin Books

PUFFIN BOOKS

Published by the Penguin Group
27 Wrights Lane, London w8 5tz, England
Viking Penguin Inc., 40 West 23rd Street, New York, New York 10010, USA
Penguin Books Australia Ltd, Ringwood, Victoria, Australia
Penguin Books Canada Ltd, 2801 John Street, Markham, Ontario, Canada l3r 1b4
Penguin Books (NZ) Ltd, 182–190 Wairau Road, Auckland 10, New Zealand

Penguin Books Ltd, Registered Offices: Harmondsworth, Middlesex, England

First published by William Heinemann Ltd 1976
Published in Puffin Books 1979
Reprinted 1981, 1983, 1988

Made and printed in Great Britain by
Richard Clay Ltd, Bungay, Suffolk
Set in Linotype Juliana

'Marvellous, isn't it?' said Niven. 'Voomy! Fantastic to think we've been on Terramare 3 for one whole year!'

'*Terr*-ah ... *ma*-ray!' said Noll, leaning forward and popping his eyes with enthusiasm. He was being old Jut-Jaw Johnson, their instructor back on Earth, more than a year ago. '"Terra" meaning earth and "Mare" meaning sea. So there you have it, lads! A planet containing both land and sea masses, a small but exciting planet!'

'Please sir, excuse me, sir,' said Niven, raising his hand and being the keen cadet. 'What about the "3", sir? It's called Terramare "3", sir, and I was wondering about the "3" –'

'Good question, Cadet!' beamed Noll, nodding his head violently in the Jut-Jaw Johnson manner. 'Glad you asked that question! Bright lad! Terramare 3 is so named, lad, because it is a land-and-sea planet of the third order. Which means that it is small in size but capable of producing certain things we need on Earth. It is also classified as a galactic trading station. All clear, Cadet?'

'No, sir, not quite sir, please sir. I thought the "3" just meant Dull, *dull* and DULL.'

'Quite right, Cadet. Terramare 3 is not just a grotty planet – not just a double-grotty planet – but a *triple-*

grotty planet. Does that answer your question, Cadet?'

'Oh yes, sir, thank you sir!' said Niven. In his own voice, he said, 'Yup. That answers my question all right ...'

He stared out at Terramare 3 through the armoured, triple-glazed hermetically sealed porthole of the tiny store-room in which he and Niven were skiving. Terramare 3 stared back, flatter than a pancake, colder than a deep-freeze, featureless as a billiards ball, relentless as a toothache, smelly as the hold of the Humper cargoship they had been unloading and cleaning out.

'Perhaps you lads,' began Noll – still being old Jut-Jaw Johnson – 'perhaps you lads are wondering what is the purpose of your mission out there in space? Well, lads, I'll tell you! You cadets are the torch-bearers of the future, the pioneers of tomorrow!'

'Ha ha,' said Niven, not laughing.

When they acted out their Jut-Jaw Johnson playlets, Niven always took the 'straight' part – the keen cadet. He looked the part. He had a 'straight' face, a determined and orderly face. His black hair grew neatly in the Regulation pattern. He was tall, disciplined-looking. The way he looked had got him nowhere. He was a Cargostripper Grade 1.

Noll's was a cartoon face. His big ears stuck out, his mouth made an O with two front teeth showing, his nose was a blob, his hair was a mat of curled copper wire. The way he looked made no difference. He was a Cargostripper Grade 1.

Noll said, 'Do you think old Jut-Jaw believed any of that splat he used to hand out to us when we were Earthside?'

'Could be. Does it matter? We believed it.'

'And here we are,' said Noll, 'all according to plan.

The pioneers. The trailblazers. Or to put it another way, Cargostrippers Grade 1, sweating away in those stinking great Humpers. Loading and unloading freight. And nothing will ever happen to change it, because nothing ever happens on Terramare 3.'

'Oh, I don't know,' said Niven. 'We'll get older. I mean, one day, we'll be grey-haired cargostrippers, genuine old veterans with bow legs and broken finger bones. We'll look back and we'll laugh –'

Su came in so quietly that they didn't even hear her. She carefully slid the door shut and said, 'Laugh? Who said laugh? I need a laugh.' She began to wriggle herself, small, slant-eyed, black and gold, between Niven and Noll. Slim as she was, it took a lot of wriggling to find any room. 'I need space,' she said, 'room to blossom and expand. I'm a free spirit –'

'Look, steady on, you're pushing me over –'

'Freedom,' she said, 'that's all I ask.'

'You've come to the right place for it,' Noll said gloomily.

'Back in Hong Kong,' she said, 'there's a restaurant looking out over the bay. They serve Pekinese-style food. Nothing gaudy, just twenty-seven dishes. I'd be wearing a gorgeous *cheongsam* split to the armpits and I'd be surrounded by handsome viddystars, not Grade 1 Cargostrippers –'

'That's back in Hong Kong,' Niven said. 'This is Terramare 3.'

'So it is,' said Su. 'Ugh.'

They stared through the porthole at the dull glitter of Terramare 3. 'Well, *something* must be happening, even here,' Su said at last. 'Anything new to report about the Wheelie?'

'Don't say that word! Don't even think it!' said

Noll, more than half seriously. He nodded at the Comm grilles above them on the wall. The whole settlement was Commed and the only time you could be sure that someone wasn't listening to you was when you were listening to someone else.

She nodded and said quietly, 'O.K. But did anything arrive for us in – you know!' She pointed in the direction of the huge Humper. You could just see the tail end of it through the window, casting double shadows from Terramare's two suns. The Humper's blaster outlets were still so hot that the cerametal tubes were changing colour all the time. Each freezing breeze painted coloured ripples on the skin of the metal. The nose of the Humper was buried in the airlock of the settlement, like a pig's nose in a trough.

'Nothing for us on the Humper,' said Niven, keeping his voice low. 'Perhaps next time ...'

'I still think you're crazy,' Su said, but nicely. 'It's such a risk ...'

At that moment, the Comm speakers came alive behind their grilles. They made a breathy, alive sound, a background noise that meant someone was using Comm to speak to someone. As long as the background noise went on, they were safe to talk in normal tones.

'We're not crazy,' said Noll. 'But we'd go crazy if we didn't have old Wheelie to think about! I mean, what else is there?'

'Old Wheelie!' said Niven dreamily. 'Just think! Once we've finished the inlet manifold gaskets and got the carburettor float sealed and –'

'Crazy!' insisted Su, but still nicely. 'Even if you really do at last finish her – smuggle in all the parts,

get them together right, actually get her ready to go –
you still can't do anything with her! You'll never start
her up, let alone *ride* her!'

'Oh yes we will,' said Noll. 'Something will happen,
somehow, sometime. You see: we'll ride her!'

'You won't,' said Su.

'Look, the Oil Ban needn't last for ever, I mean it's
only a law and laws are made to be broken –'

'Not that law,' said Su. 'Look, I work in RadRec, I've
seen the records. I *know*.'

Noll, suddenly angry, said, 'Just because you've got
a soft job sitting in front of a Records console doesn't
mean –'

Su said, 'You're asking for trouble. You can't and
won't get round the Oil Ban.'

'Why not?' Noll demanded. 'Tell me why not!'

'All right, I will. I'll give you a history lesson. It
starts in nineteen-eighty-something. I was watching
that year only last week, after hours –'

'Against the law!' Niven interrupted. 'You're not
allowed to use RadRec viddy material for personal
reasons! But you did – which proves the law can be
broken!'

'I was watching that year,' Su said. 'Just one year.
Supertankers splitting open, oil slicks hundreds of
miles long, dead fish, dead birds, everything dead. And
the oil wars, I watched them. Some nations were getting too rich because they had oil, others were getting
poorer and poorer and turning nastier and nastier.
Pollution in the seas, great traffic jams in the cities, a
really big war was coming up –'

'And so we got the Oil Ban,' Noll said. 'But I still
like Wheelie. I still want to see her go, hear her go –'

'I don't see how they made the Oil Ban work,' Niven said. 'I mean they had to have oil, everything was dependent on oil.'

'Rad,' Noll said. 'Rad. You didn't listen at school, did you?'

'They got Rad more or less working in 1992,' Su said. 'They could beam a whole continent by then. And by the end of the 1990s, they'd really got it going. Rad world-wide! So the Oil Ban *could* work. And today, my old grannie in Kowloon buys a toothbrush, codes in to Rad and – buzz! – clean teeth! Heat a house, drive a Humper, warm the bathwater, run this yatty settlement – all you've got to do is code into Rad. It's everywhere, like a web over the whole Galaxy! So who needs oil and petrol?'

'I do!' said Noll. 'I need them for old Wheelie!'

Silence for a moment. Then Su went back to the attack.

'What's so voomy about old Wheelie?' she said. 'I mean ... you're obsessed with her! What's she *for*? What's the *good* of her?'

'What do you mean, what's the good of her?' said Niven. 'It's obvious! She's – she's the Wheelie! She's the ultimate maximost! I mean, look at it our way, Su –'

'I do look at it your way! What could you have done without me? Nothing! Who took the risks and used RadRec to get you the manual? Me! Who sewed that splatty old saddle? Me! Look at my fingers!'

'Ooops!' said Noll, patting the small hand. 'Sorry! Of course we couldn't have managed without you!'

'What I meant was,' Niven said, 'look at old Wheelie for what she is. Gorgeous! Wonderful! Voomy! Last word!'

'I can't look at her,' Su said, still more than half angry. 'There's nothing to look at. You haven't finished her and the way you're going you never will. Nothing on the last Humper, nothing on this Humper. Your friends back home are scared splatty. And you two, you're just dreaming!'

'Well, it's difficult for them at Earthside too,' said Noll. 'I mean, what we're doing is smuggling. The worst sort of smuggling.'

'You're not doing it very well,' Su said sulkily. 'You're just dreamers.'

'What's so bad about a dream?' Noll said. 'What's so great about life on Terramare 3? Why shouldn't Niven and I have fun with old Wheelie? Who's going to –'

Niven said, 'Shut up! Listen!' He jabbed his finger frantically at the Comm grille. The background noise wasn't there any more. The loudspeaker was completely silent. Niven went white. Su whispered, 'It's probably O.K. ... There was probably nobody listening ...'

But then the Comm came alive again and a voice said, 'Loaders 13M and 15M report instantly to Controller, Personnel Section. Also Records 5F, report instantly to Controller, Personnel Section. I repeat –'

While the voice repeated the message, Loader 13M, who was Noll, got slowly to his feet. He did not look at Loader 15M, who was Niven; nor at Records 5F, whose golden skin had gone a putty colour. They did not speak as they made their own way down the evenly lit corridors to Control. Personnel Section.

The Controller's name was Banna. They had seen him, studied him and classified him as a Yessir Beaver

Grade 1. Which meant that he was one of the authorities who always said, 'Yes, sir!' to the high-ups; worked like a beaver; and was a Grade 1 menace. The sort of person who consults Regulations before blowing his nose.

Banna sat with a copy of the Regulations on his desk and a handkerchief in his hand. This should have been funny, but wasn't.

He was wiping his bald brown head with the handkerchief and prodding miserably at a Comm memoboard. They had time to study him. He was small, goggle-eyed, bony as a starving rat and somehow dried up. Just as you would expect of a Yessir Beaver Grade 1, he pretended not to notice them for some time and went on with his prodding. At last he looked up and asked a question that amazed them. He *should* have said, 'What were you three doing, during duty hours, in an off-limits store cupboard?' What he did say, in his nervous, high-pitched voice, was 'Can any of you work the "erase" on this thing?'

Su took the Comm memoboard from him. She said, 'You just press "Erase" and "Function" both at the same time. You were only pressing –'

'Oh yes, oh yes,' Banna said, wiping his forehead again. 'Of course! ... They make these things too small.'

He ran out of things to say and began pulling at his face, twisting his nose, his forehead, his chin. They stared at him and suddenly realized what was wrong with him. He was terrified.

'Personnel of my grade,' he said, 'are not allowed to erase anything. *Anything at all.* Did you know that?'

They said they hadn't known that (and, in fact, they hadn't).

'Well, watch this!' said Banna. Two bony fingertips pressed two tiny buttons. The memoboard winked once or twice. Banna picked up his handkerchief, groaned, and mopped his head.

'There!' he said. 'Now you've got to trust me!'

Su looked a question at Noll, who lifted his eyebrows at Niven, who shrugged. Banna looked from face to face, as if expecting someone to say something. Nobody did.

'But don't you understand?' Banna cried. 'It's all right! It's safe! No one knows that I've called you in here, or about the store-room, or anything – you can see for yourself, I can Comm any part of the settlement, any single room, even that store-room –' He poked at the Comm, trying to prove that he meant what he said. 'No one heard what I said to you over the Comm!' he continued. 'Unless there was a fourth person in that store-room with you! There wasn't, was there?' he pleaded.

'No. Just us three.'

'And now I've wiped out even the record of that Comm call!' said Banna, eyes popping. 'I've erased! We're *safe*, don't you see? So you can tell me all about it!'

'About W H A T?' shouted Noll. 'I don't know what you're raving on about!'

Banna fell back in his chair, staring at Noll. 'About Wheelie, of course!' he said. 'I want to know all about Wheelie! I want to join you, help build her, get her running!'

After a long, stunned silence, Niven said, 'I don't

believe you. You're lying. You're putting us on.'

Instead of answering, Banna violently pulled open a drawer – scrabbled inside it – and produced a small sealed bottle. He rolled it across his desk to Niven. 'Open it!'

Niven opened it. It was full of a clear fluid.

'Smell it!'

Niven smelled it, shrugged, and passed it to Noll. Noll put his nose to the bottle and said, 'All right, it smells. There is a strong smell. Is that all?'

Banna, squeaking again, said, 'You mean, you don't know what that fluid is? You don't know that smell?'

'It's just another rotten smell,' said Noll.

But Su sniffed the bottle and said, 'Go on, Mr Banna! Tell us!'

'It's *petrol!*' Banna yelped. 'Petrol, petrol, petrol! The lifeblood of that machine of yours! Petrol! I made it myself ... *And I can make more!*'

'Petrol ... !' whispered Noll. 'But that's illegal! Owning that little bottle could finish you!'

'So you must believe me! Believe I am your friend! You must accept me!'

Noll looked at Niven. Niven looked at Su. She shrugged, then nodded.

'All right,' said Noll. 'You're in, Mr Banna.'

The little brown man let out a great breath of air, sat back in his chair and smiled.

'Tell me about Wheelie,' he said. 'Tell me *everything!*'

Noll said, 'She's a motorbike. A very good one. What was called a Vincent Black Shadow –'

'I know that, I know that!' Banna cried. 'Vincent HRD, twin-cylinder, 1000 cc, high camshafts. You mustn't treat me like a fool!'

'But how did you know?' Noll said, shaken.

'How do you think?' said Banna. 'Su found it possible to use RadRec! And then there is Comm. I have listened to you three talking – oh, a dozen times, twenty times ... even when you were unloading Humpers I listened to you. You have been such fools. Taking such terrible risks with your mouths. It must stop, we must protect Wheelie!'

'Look, why are you so keen about Wheelie? What does she matter to you?' said Niven.

Banna looked at him disgustedly. 'You have no imagination,' he said. 'I am eighty. Now, *think*. How old was I when the Oil Ban started? Yes, you are right, I was a tiny little boy. And I was in an Indian village. There was a doctor who came to us, he was a great man; we counted off the months till he was due. Then we would hear the roaring of his motorbike, a long way away. It would come nearer! – and then the doctor was with us, there were people running and laughing and crowding round the doctor. But for me, there was only the motorbike. I squatted in the brown dust in front of it, staring at it.

'And one day the doctor took me for a ride on this wonderful motorbike of his. A Velocette. We roared over the dusty, bumpy roads, I burned my ankle on the exhaust pipe, I clung to the doctor like a little monkey!

'And when I got off the motorbike, I said to myself, "One day I will leave this village: leave it on a motorbike. I will ride off to the new, modern world, hidden from the past in a cloud of swirling dust! I will become a great man, a scientific man!"'

'And did you?' said Su quietly.

Banna shrugged his narrow shoulders. 'There were

the oil wars, and soldiers pushing at us with their stupid guns ... A *peace* force, with *guns!* I left my village on foot, carrying a bundle bigger than myself for endless miles, surrounded by people moaning and complaining and sometimes dying. And then there was the Oil Ban. And then I went to England and Japan and America and qualified to be what I am to-day – a Controller of Personnel on Terramare 3!' He was twisting his nose, hard. 'But I want that motor-bike still!' he said. 'I want it because I *want* it! A machine made for one man, a machine with power to control –'

'You can't have Wheelie,' Noll said. 'She's ours.'

Banna looked at him and laughed. 'I am eighty. I told you that. They think I am only seventy-two, but I am eighty. That is quite old. I may not live another twenty years – and they will retire me in three years. I do not want to *own* the Wheelie; I do not want to *ride* her, even. That would be stupid. But I want to share the adventure of her! And I will. You can do nothing without me.'

'Petrol?' said Noll.

'Yes, petrol. I *made* that petrol,' said Banna. 'I made it here! In our own laboratories! I refined it from the oil I stole from the Humpers –'

'Oil from the *Humpers*? You mean, we still use oil? But the Oil Ban –'

'Oh dear me,' said Banna wearily. 'The galaxy runs on Rad – and oil. Yes, oil! *Lubricating* oil, don't you see? Vegetable oils mostly, but sometimes mineral oil, the old forbidden sort of oil! Machines must be *lubricated*. Oil *lubricates*. Isn't it obvious?'

'Laws were made to be broken!' Niven murmured to Su.

'Only at top level,' she replied.

Banna said, 'From oil I got petrol. I can make more. I will make more. Right. How far have you got with Wheelie? Tell me precisely.'

They told him. Banna wrote a list.

Noll said, 'Isn't that dangerous, that list you're making?'

Banna said, 'The list goes here!' and tapped his forehead. He stared at the list, brown forehead puckered, for a half a minute; then threw it in the eater. The eater whirred.

'You have no tyres,' he said. 'That is the worst thing. The rest doesn't matter. Su has finished the saddle, there are many small mechanical things to see to, the frame is complete, the spokes of the wheels are sound – you are sure of that? – and you got high and low tension leads on the last Humper ...'

Niven said, 'That's the worst bit, the electrics.'

Banna said, 'The timing might be difficult in spite of the manual. We need experience. But we could use Rad for the electrics ... I could code in to the Rad module. People of my grade are allowed coders. I have half a dozen here in my desk drawer and more in the safe.'

'But you can't just open up the Radball and stick in a dozen coders!' said Niven. 'It's impossible! The module is – is *holy*, nobody's allowed near it!'

'What do you know about the Rad module, the Radball?' said Banna.

Noll said, 'I don't know anything about Rad modules except what we were taught when we were cadets. They told us that Earth has got Radballs all over the place to pick up the Rad power web and redistribute it ... and small settlements like this one

17

have one Radball to power everything ... That's all I know.'

Banna leaned backwards and tapped out a code on the Comm. From the grille, a voice said, 'Regulations concerning the location of the Rad Module on settlements of the third order. One : there shall be a single module, Type Omnifunction 3 L D all-purpose, to be situated not farther than 300 metres and not closer than 250 metres from the Central Control Offices of the Settlement and not farther than 500 metres and not closer than 450 metres from the Habitation Zones and not farther than –'

Banna cut the Comm and said, 'Well? Have you seen a Radball situated not farther than 300 metres and not closer than 250 metres anywhere around here?'

'No,' said Su.

'I haven't seen our Radball at all,' said Niven. 'In fact, I don't even know what it looks like !'

'It's a sphere, a ball, about the size of this room,' said Banna. 'And it's completely sealed against interference. Or should be. And it's supposed to be close to the settlement. But it isn't.'

'Why not?' Su asked.

'Disregard of the Regulations. When this planet was first settled, they landed almost on the other side. They started building a Regulation settlement. Halfway through – well, you know the surface of Terramare 3. Frozen sea and sand, with a thin crust of ice. Frozen land, much of it sand or quicksand, with the same thin crust of ice. Halfway through the building, they found they'd picked the wrong place. The settlement began to sink. So they did a better survey, found a better site, and built the settlement here.'

'And left the Radball where it was?'

'That's right. The Radball was never re-located. It's out there, three hundred kilometres away.'

'But isn't it your duty to do something?' said Noll, looking closely at Banna. 'I mean, you're a high-up, and you know the Regulations ...'

'I'm a Personnel Officer,' Banna shrugged. 'And I have a hobby. I make petrol. I made the petrol in that bottle. I made it with Rad power to drive RadMech tools. With Rad power to work the refining plant. With RadRec information to tell me what to do next. Look out of the window: look at the tyres on my Doughnut.'

Niven got up and looked. Banna's Doughnut was crusted with ice all along the lower sides of its body. Its fat, doughnut tyres were worn. The plexiglass of the air-conditioned cabin was filthy. The other Doughnuts were clean.

Niven said, 'You've hardly got any tread left on those tyres.'

Banna said, 'That's right. I've been through three sets since I got her. I'm always out in my Doughnut. The others think I'm mad. I tell them I'm prospecting, exploring the planet. But the real reason why I go out so often in the Doughnut is that it gives me the excuse to go to the Rad module; and slip another code in, whenever I need to.'

'And the Commanding Officer has never noticed?'

'The Commanding Officer has other things on his mind,' said Banna drily. 'He has to sit still for very long periods with his eyes closed, to think about these matters. But never mind about him. What matters to me and you is – Wheelie.'

They sat silent for a while. Then Banna said, 'I'd like to see Wheelie. I've got an idea for making the tyres. Can I see her?'

Noll, Niven and Su looked at each other worriedly. Then Noll said, 'I suppose so. Yes.'

They'd hidden Wheelie in the simplest, most obvious place; the nastiest cell in the smelliest corner of the Humper loading cellars.

The cellars were the biggest thing in the settlement. They supported all the buildings above ground and provided storage for incoming and outgoing cargoes. They housed the heating and air-conditioning plant, the guts of the plumbing, RadRec, RadMech stores, communications and everything else needed. The cellars were supposed to be regularly inspected and tidied, always organized and orderly. They were nothing of the sort. They were a cluttered mess.

Niven pulled aside a huge packing case and nodded the others forward. Niven pulled the packing case shut behind them, then tackled another heap of cases, drums and discarded containers.

A wheel showed. Chromium glinted sharply. The black tubes of the girder front forks gleamed. Banna said, 'Ah ...!'

Niven pulled aside the rest of the rubbish, and there she was: low-seated, arrogantly bulged round her petrol tank, delicately finned round her cylinders, infinitely complicated. She seemed to say, 'I am quiet now. Unmoving. But there's a curved, boomerang-like lever sticking out of my side. If you kicked that lever, I would come alive. I'd roar and click and whirr and bellow and throb for you. And if you pulled this lever here, and kicked that other pedal there, and twisted the grip under your hand, I'd give a slight jerk as my hidden mysteries meshed ... And if you opened your fingers, slowly and gently, over the lever – and twisted that worn grip a little more – I'd go forward, very slowly, a very little way, pulsing and thundering contentedly, just clearing my throat, just awaiting your pleasure ...

'And moments later, I'd tear the wind against your face and pull the muscles of your arms and ram my rear wheel up your spine.'

Banna's face was expressionless. He just stood there, looking. He stood so long that Noll muttered, 'Something wrong with her?'

Banna let loose a long sigh and said, 'Even in her day – even when there were thousands, millions, of machines like her – people would have stopped to look at her. Clustered round her. "A Vincent HRD!" they'd have said. "And what a Vincent HRD!"'

Then he said, 'Tyres. It's better than I hoped. You've got the originals. Oh, they're no good, of course, look at them! But they give us the pattern ...' He started talking to himself about carbon fibres and extrusions of poly-something and RadMech.

'Can you make them?' Noll said.

'Oh yes! And better than the originals. Better than rubber and fibre, much better ...'

He was off again. Su, Noll and Niven looked at each other, smiling. Then they put their arms round each others' shoulders and began quietly to jig around in a circle. Banna took no notice. He squatted by the Wheelie and his lips moved as he dictated notes to his brain.

*

Two days later, the Comm said, 'Records 5F report to Controller, Personnel Section. I repeat –'

Su went to Banna's office. He said, 'Come in. I can't ask the boys; it wouldn't be safe. You're from Records, I've got a reason for talking to you. You've got to remember everything and tell them. Right?'

She said, 'I'm the go-between. Right.'

'The tyres,' he said. 'It's going to work. Give the boys this.' He threw a horseshoe section of greyish stuff across the desk and rubbed his thin brown hands together.

'Congratulate me!' he piped, chuckling and hunching his shoulders. He looked like a happy brown gnome.

She said, 'Congratulations,' and got up to go.

He said, 'No, stay. Tell me something. How did Noll and Niven get hold of Wheelie?'

'Oh, it started years ago when Noll and Niven were cadets on Earth. An old house was pulled down. One of the demolition team was a seventeen-year-old friend of Noll's, or Niven's, I can't remember which. Anyhow, the house had cellars and when they got to the cellars they found old Wheelie. She was *walled in*. Bricked up. Mummified. Every bit of her was covered in some grease or other, pelonium jelly –'

'– petroleum jelly. Go on.'

'There was plastic sheeting over her too. The demolition boy wasn't very interested but Noll and Niven were. They went down into the cellar one night with spanners and everything, and took Wheelie to pieces. They had a flashcam, they snapped everything before, during and after they took it down. And it all grew from there. They went mad about Wheelie and when they stopped being cadets and came here as Cargo-strippers, they smuggled her in, bit by bit, on the Humpers.'

'Through their contacts on Earth?'

'All sorts of contacts! They've got –' She stopped, and put her hand to her mouth.

Banna said, 'Don't worry, Su. It's too late to worry, I know too much. And anyhow I'm on your side. I can tell you the rest. I can guess it all. They've got contacts who put things on the Humpers whenever they can; and they must have had – still have – friends on Earth who look for useful bits and pieces ... old electrical bits like headlamp bulbs. Brass unions. And information, of course –'

'I got most of the information,' said Su. 'I got it straight off RadRec. The Manual, road tests, articles from those funny old motorcycling magazines, all kinds of stuff.'

'I envy you,' Banna said. 'It must have been fascinating.'

'It was risky. If I'd been found ...'

She bit her lip, then shrugged and said, 'I keep wondering about the man who mummified her in that cellar.'

'I can tell you about him!' Banna said. 'In fact, I can almost see him! He wasn't a young man, he couldn't have been very young. A Vincent H R D was already a valuable antique when the Oil Ban came into force. Only someone with quite a lot of money could have bought her – or even wanted to buy her, perhaps. No, I see a middle-aged man, very determined, crazy about machines and motorbikes. He's saved his money, bought the Wheelie, spent every penny he had on making her perfect. He finishes his job and comes back to her. He polishes this, adjusts that, smooths out the ports, fiddles with the carbs ...'

'You're as bad as he was!' said Su.

'... And at last, he's got her perfect. Then – slam! – down comes Authority with the Oil Ban! No more petrol engines of any kind, not even for lawnmowers and lighting generators! Everything's got to be Rad-powered. So our man says to himself, "Here's one piece of machinery the Oil Ban isn't going to destroy!" Perhaps he takes her out on the road and has a final fling with her. No, perhaps not; if the Authority saw him, they'd confiscate her. They confiscated everything, you know! Everything that used oil and petrol. Even paraffin lamps and things like that.'

'Paraffin lamps? What were they?'

'Never mind. Our man puts the Wheelie in the cellar. He drains this, flushes that, protects the other. As you say, he mummifies her. He thinks, perhaps one day they'll lift the Oil Ban, and then ... But they don't. The man dies, and Noll and Niven find old Wheelie.'

Su said, 'I'd better get back. What do you want me to tell the boys?'

'Tell them the tyres will be all right.'

'But they're not supposed to be grey, they're black –'

'Don't worry about that, that's just pigment. I can give them black tyres. Tell them I've got the wire-braced extrusion right.'

'When will they be ready? Oh, and what about the tubes? They say they've got to have tubes inside the tyres; I don't know what they mean but that's what they say.'

'Tell them no, these are tubeless. I've got a way of

sealing the spokeholes. Oh, and another thing. Tell them we'll have dual ignition.'

'Dual ignition?'

'That's right. Ignition by Rad, and the proper Vincent system as well. Are you sure you can remember all this?'

'Of course I can. I'm not stupid, you know. I know quite a lot about old Wheelie. I know they want the proper ignition system, they don't want Rad stuff. It wouldn't be original. They keep talking about it, "Everything must be original" ...'

Banna said, 'They don't understand. Rad is simple, the old electrical systems were very difficult ...'

Su said, 'I'd better go.'

'You're sure you can remember it all?' he said worriedly.

'Yes. You're a strange man, Mr Banna.'

'I'm a madman, Su. Like Noll and Niven. Mad.'

Even in the Centre, they didn't feel completely safe. The Centre was cafeteria, viddy room, assembly hall, gymnasium, theatre, lounge, all in one. The cafeteria part was permanent, the other parts were pulled out of walls, rose through floors, dropped from ceilings, as need arose. Anyone in the settlement could use the Centre. Everyone was supposed to use it for meals, even the Commanding Officer (but he didn't, of course: somehow it always turned out that he was too busy).

'We're seen together too much,' Noll said to Niven. All around them in the Centre, people were eating, talking, playing. One man was even smoking. He stood right by the aircon so that the smoke from his Synthaciggy was sucked out straight away.

Banna joined them. He seemed relaxed. He was not pulling his face about. Noll said, 'I was just saying: we're seen together too much. What do you think?'

Banna said, 'Don't worry about it,' but he started twisting the skin on his forehead. 'The other day,' he said to Su, 'your Chief came up to me and said "Glad to see you mixing with the kids. Good for them, good for you, good for the settlement!"'

'Yes, but it's always us – you, me, Su, Niven. That's suspicious.'

'Play you golf,' Niven said, rising and pulling Su to her feet. 'The table's free. Come on.' They went to the golf course, put one Galac in the slot and teed off.

Su laughed and said, 'You always do that, Niven! You always squint like that!' but he didn't hear, he was concentrating on getting the white dot of the golf ball just exactly right before bringing the whole weight of his fingertip down on the club. Click! Straight up the fairway, and a read-out of 1.3 for the approach shot.

He grinned and said, 'Championship stuff! Voomy!'

She said, 'You've got this table fixed!' and scored a poor 2.4. He putted and watched the big close-up get bigger still as his ball teetered on the edge of the hole and dropped in. 'Stupid game!' Su said, grinning. Back at the table Noll said to Banna, 'Tell me more about the old days. More about – you know.'

Banna flicked his eyes round the room and wished he hadn't. It was the ViddyComm that mattered, the little television eyes in the walls. Human eyes were nothing to them. He twisted his nose and said, 'They were everywhere when I was a kid. I can remember all the names, all of them. Honda, Suzuki, Yamaha, Kawasaki – all Japanese. Gilera and Moto-Guzzi from Italy, Harley Davidson from America, C Z and M Z from the old communist bloc in eastern Europe … Puch, Laverda, Mobylette, B M W – all kinds of machines, all sizes, all shapes, two-strokes and four-strokes, they were everywhere. Even some old British machines. Norton, Triumph, B S A, Velocette –'

Noll said, 'It must have been massive! Just seeing them! All those machines roaring along, all those helmeted riders jetting off to wherever they wanted to go! Everyone watching them go by, cheering them on!'

Banna sighed and said, 'You've got it all wrong. You won't listen, you won't understand. They were just motorbikes, just one more thing on the roads. And the roads weren't what you think, they weren't *adventures*, they were just roads with signs on them saying HALT and GIVE WAY, and Do This and Don't Do That and Stop At the Lights.'

'You make it sound like today,' said Noll sulkily.

'It *was* like today – today back on Earth – only noisier, smellier, more dangerous. Instead of doing a silent 20 max – miles an hour, that is – those machines could do 100. That means, say, 160 kph! And you didn't just sit astride them like you sit on your Moppet, you had to drive them; really drive them. People were very competitive then, even on the roads.'

'And the noise, and the smell … ,' said Noll dreamily. He thought of his Moppet, a fat-tyred, plexi-shielded, two-wheeled Rad-mobile. It was all he was allowed, all anyone of his Grade was allowed. It whimpered and whined its way over anything within the permitted 30 kilometre radius of the settlement (the drive just cut out if you tried to go beyond 30 km). It took the salt flats of Terramare 3 in its slow stride, the fat tyres changing shape to keep their tender grip on the ice slick, its invisible power unit, part of the rear wheel, endlessly working things out for itself. He remembered when his Moppet refused to go any farther across a stretch of soft ice-sand. It had worked it all out and said to itself, 'No, I think not: not quite *safe.*'

He thought of the Wheelie, black and silver with a flourish of gold on the muscled bulge of the tank, and the complexity of her, and the challenge you saw whenever you looked at her.

'Tell me about the Vincents!' he said.

Banna said, 'Keep your voice down! I've told you before, I was very young then. A little boy. I only saw the most obvious things – the Hondas and Suzukis and Yamahas. I never saw a Vincent HRD, not ever. Or if I did, I never knew of it.'

'But if they were so good, everyone must have wanted them!'

'Everyone didn't get what they wanted. It was the same then as now. What most people wanted was something like your Moppet – a machine that would just go, not stop, not give trouble, get them there and back.'

'But you said everything moved faster then, you said people drove competitively –'

'Don't raise your voice.'

'It's just that thinking about old Wheelie, I get so –'

'I'll play you golf. Come on.'

They got up and joined the queue to play golf. Niven and Su were just finishing. She'd fluked her way through the course and was giggling: she might even win. Noll watched Niven frowning at the machine, twitching his backside as he set up his drive for the last hole, poising his finger over the key. But in Niven's mind the little Viddygolf screen became an endless road and he was rushing along it, crouched low over the tank, the handlebars pulling at his arms and the wind at his goggles; and old Wheelie was charging into the landscape, the road was tearing past him, she was *eating* the ribbon of roads ...

Su was nudging him. She was laughing and saying, 'Hey! Hey! I won! Well, nearly ... Well, I should have won!'

When they got back to their table all their seats were taken so they stood and watched the viddy walls. The programme was mostly official stuff. Dull.

Two weeks later, they made another pilgrimage to old Wheelie. They pulled away the rubbish that hid her and just stood there, looking. Then Banna reached into the pocket of his white coat and pulled out a mechanism that filled his hand.

'Rad ignition!' he said. 'Replaces all the old stuff! You can wire it to the distributor if you like or – on this circuit here, you pull the lever over – straight to the plugs.'

'Voomy!' said Noll, but his voice was uncertain.

Niven said, 'Great!' after a pause that was a little too long.

'Don't you see,' Banna said, 'the old gear is difficult. I mean it's simple – but not for us. Not if we want to get it completely right. But with this, we can read off the performance on a MechElec and *know* we've got it right. You see what I mean, don't you?'

Noll and Niven were silent.

At last Niven said, 'I'm sorry, but no. It's not *original*. It's not *right*.'

Su murmured, 'I told you so, Mr Banna!'

Banna said, 'But we could spend hours – days – trying to get the original electrics working as they should, and never succeed!'

Su interrupted, 'And you won't have hours or days. It's got to be right the very first time. Which could be the only time you ever see or hear old Wheelie actually running! I mean, once you start up, everyone in the settlement will know. The Comm will pick her up electronically. And there'll be the noise as well.'

Noll said, 'I'm against it,' and stuck out his lower lip.

Banna said, 'Well. Well ... All right then. If you insist. If you insist. We'll use the original stuff. But you know the trouble we had with the suspension and the double clutch. If we get the ignition wrong –'

Noll and Niven said nothing. They worked on the Wheelie and watched Banna out of the corners of their eyes as he fussily, efficiently, fiddled with the HT leads and crude little electrical mechanisms.

'He knows what he's doing,' Noll whispered to Niven.

Half an hour later Banna said, 'That's it. She'd run.'

'She'd *run?*' said Noll. 'Actually go?'

'I've faked the battery with a PowerPak. Not original, but – !'

'She'd *run?*' Noll repeated.

'You really mean that?' said Niven. His voice was hollow, like Noll's.

'I really mean it,' said Banna.

'Hell ...' whispered Noll. 'She'd actually *go* ...'

*

That evening, in the Centre, Su said, 'Trouble!'

Noll and Niven went on filling their plates with food from the dispensers and Noll said, 'What kind of trouble?' Su made a face that meant, 'Wait a minute! Can't talk here!' They waited until they had found a safe place, in the noisiest part of the Centre.

Niven said, 'Something to do with old Wheelie?'

She said, 'Could be. I don't know yet. But a HiPri came through this afternoon –'

'A *what*?'

'A HiPri. A High Priority order from Galactic Command, Earth. A message, stupid. I'm not supposed to know what comes in and out of RadRec, but I have my ways . . . Anyway, the C O's out.'

'The Commanding Officer? Kicked out?'

'Posted, anyhow.'

'Well . . . !' Noll said. 'What did he do?' Then, remembering where he was, he stopped looking surprised and concentrated on eating his food.

'It's what he didn't do,' Niven said. 'Never does a thing. Never puts in an appearance.'

'Anyhow, he's out,' Su said. 'And that could mean trouble.'

'Why trouble? What trouble?' Noll said.

'The new C O is called Bannister,' she said, talking into her plate, very quietly. 'Also known as Bang-Bang Bannister. Hard man. Campaign medals. Discipline man. Bang-Bang, you're dead.'

'So what? How does that make any difference to old Wheelie?'

'There's things called Regulations,' Su said. 'They tell you how a settlement should be run. Ours isn't run according to Regulations, you may have noticed.

When Bang-Bang comes, there'll be a clean-up. New broom in every nook and cranny of this splatty old settlement.'

'Oh,' said Noll sickly.

'I see,' said Niven, stopping eating. 'You mean, he might dig right down to the loading cellars?'

Su said nothing, but Noll said, 'He might not bother to. I mean, who cares about the loading cellars?'

Niven said, 'Oh well . . . We'll have to wait and see.'

'I don't think we ought to wait,' Noll answered. 'I think we ought to get down there and really finish her. Get her absolutely right, as soon as possible. How long have we got, Su?'

'A day. He arrives within forty-eight hours.'

'A day! But that's not long enough –'

'I don't know why you're panicking,' Niven said. 'After all, Bang-Bang might be all right. Everything might work out fine . . .'

Next day there was a roar in the sky that wasn't a Humper. It was Bang-Bang Bannister's very own Sola Invader, flown and navigated by him. The Sola had been a combat craft and still looked tough.

Two minutes after he landed, there was another roar. It came from Bang-Bang himself. He had noticed some dust behind a Comm grille.

Two hours later, all personnel were assembled in the Centre. Everyone looked wide-eyed and tight-mouthed.

Bang-Bang made his entrance. He was six foot two inches tall, sandy-haired and about eighty. Some of him – the creases on his face, the horny shine of his big ears – looked ninety: but the rest of him looked sixty at most. You could tell that the bits that looked sixty were the bits that did damage in any sort of argument.

There was silence while he took off his zap jacket – he did not wear uniform – kicked over a canteen table and rubbed the underneath of the tabletop with the Galaxy patch on the jacket. He examined the emblem carefully and said, in a voice like sticks breaking, 'You have insulted the emblem of the Galaxy. LOOK!' He thrust the emblem into the nose of a viddy scanner and a big picture of the emblem loomed up on the viddyscreens. There was, quite definitely, a slight stain on the emblem.

Nobody said anything.

'I have news for you all,' said Bang-Bang Bannister. 'I have a present for you. A gift. I am going to give you two days. Two whole days! But that,' he added, in a very low crackle, 'is all I'm going to give you! Forty-eight hours and then –'

Everyone held their breath.

'– And then,' he continued, 'I inspect. I inspect. And I expect. DISMISS!'

He was gone. People breathed. Noll said, 'Goodbye, old Wheelie!' Niven shrugged his shoulders. They went to the Humper bay and began cleaning things. Anything. Everything. The more they cleaned, the more the packing cases that hid old Wheelie stood out.

Noll said, 'We've got to think. Really think. What can we do with her? Where can we hide her?'

'Wait a minute!' Niven said. 'I've had an idea! A voomy idea! What's the dirtiest thing in this splatty cellar?'

'Me,' said Noll, looking at his hands.

'No! Better than that! Try again!'

'The elephant trunk!' Noll shouted. He kicked the elephant trunk. It went, 'Boi-O I-oi-Oi-oi-O I N G!' along its whole length, echoing and re-echoing dismally.

'You're right, lad, right!' Niven beamed. 'It's so foul, so splatty, that even Bang-Bang doesn't expect it to be clean! He'll look *at* it but he'd never look *into* it, right?'

Noll kicked the trunk gently, listening to its dim, thundering echo. The trunk was an enormous jointed tube 80 metres long and two metres high. It led from the Humper bay direct to the settlement's air-conditioner. When you stop a Humper, you give its motor compartments a blast-through: when you've finished unloading it, you give the cargo compartment a blast through. The filth and fumes go through the elephant's trunk and are eaten or neutralized by the air-conditioner.

Noll said, 'What happens if a Humper arrives?'

'We'll get Su to give us the schedule. We're not due for another Humper for just under two weeks.'

'But if one did arrive, and blasted-through – and Wheelie was in there –'

'Which would you rather: Bang-Bang finds Wheelie, or we take a chance?'

Noll said nothing. He got tools and started undoing the huge circlips that held one section of trunking to another. Niven silently joined him in the work.

In half an hour, they had two circlips loose and the section could be manhandled and rolled to one side. 'Quietly. We don't want anyone to hear it rolling. Get those packing case liners, the soft ones . . .'

The cylindrical section rolled aside over the liners spread on the floor. There was very little noise, just a soft DOOOOM, DOOOOM. But the section left a dusty mess.

They got Wheelie and wheeled her into the trunk. She felt smooth and heavy and powerful, even being wheeled. The new tyres cut a sharp pattern in the black dust on the ground. When she was in, she glinted at them from the gloom of the tube. Noll sighed. Niven said, 'Let's finish off, then,' and they began rolling the section back.

And then there were fast footsteps, and a throat being cleared with a sound like twigs breaking – and Bang-Bang was there with a swagger stick in his hand and the two big SecSecs, Security Section men, at his side.

Bang-Bang snapped, 'What are you doing?'

Noll said, 'Cleaning up, sir. Cleaning everything, sir.' His voice went into a squeak: he saw Wheelie's tyre marks on the black dust.

Niven saw them too. He said, 'Everything, sir! Cleaning everything!' and he bent down – picked up packing-case liners – swept them about to wipe out the tyre marks – began piling the liners on top of each other. Even his big ears were scarlet.

Bang-Bang said, 'You! Have you ever read Regulations?'

Niven said, 'Yes, sir. At Cadet School, sir.'

'What do Regulations say about men of your grade and this trunking?' He hit the trunk with his swagger stick: it went DA-ANG-ANG! as if hurt.

'Don't know, sir!' Niven said.

Noll said, 'Not part of our duties to see to the trunking sir. But –'

'But what?'

'But it was leaking, sir. And it's no good cleaning if

the trunking's leaking, sir. So we repaired the join where the leak was, sir!'

'Leaking?' said Bang-Bang. He leaned forward and stared into Noll's face.

'Leaking, sir,' said Noll. 'Look, sir, you can see the dirt!'

Bang-Bang lowered his head and looked. There was still just a trace of Wheelie's tyre mark. Noll could recognize it. Would Bang-Bang? Noll sweated.

Bang-Bang said, 'Good. Initiative shown. Continue clearing this mess.' Noll and Niven breathed again. But then Bang-Bang said, 'Keep away from the trunking in future. Don't tamper with it.'

He turned to one of the SecSec men and said, 'Put this on report: trunking not properly maintained. Find out who's responsible. Reprimand him. Understood and noted.'

'Keep away from the trunking,' Bang-Bang snapped to Niven and Noll. He strode off.

When they could speak, Niven said, 'He'd got a swagger stick ...! He carried a swagger stick! I've heard of them, but never seen one. An actual swagger stick ...!'

Noll said, 'Now what do we do? We're finished. So's old Wheelie.'

Niven said, 'We'll find a way, somehow. We can't just leave her in the trunking ...'

'This place is Commed, we don't dare go near the trunking. It's all finished! We've locked her in here and we can't get her out!'

Niven began to swear.

That evening, three young men were waiting for them as they left the Centre. They were General

Duties – which included cleaning. The biggest of the three said, 'You two. You put us right in the splat, didn't you? Messing about with the trunking!'

Before he knew what was happening, Niven was doubled up, choking, clutching his stomach. The big one had hit him fast and hard. The other two grabbed Noll and the big one punched him in the stomach until he was sick. 'You want to keep away from that trunking,' the big one said.

Later, Su said, 'You're not going to let that stop you, are you?'

'Oh, no!' said Noll bitterly. 'I mean, what is there to stop us? Just Bang-Bang this morning, then those three giving us a beating up. Oh no, the future's rosy. Everything's voomy.'

'But you can't give up!' said Su.

'I can,' Niven said. 'Just you watch. I can give up, just like that.'

'Me too,' said Noll. 'I've had enough, thank you. Enough.'

'But –' Su began.

'Out of my way,' Niven said. 'I'm going to be sick again.'

Next day, they told Banna what had happened. He hardly heard them. He was so frightened that they could only just get sense out of him. His voice, always high, was now frozen into a permanent squeak. His eyes were like ping-pong balls.

He and his department had been inspected by Bang-Bang.

'About Wheelie,' Noll said.

Banna answered with a small yelp and a jump, as if he were a mouse and the cat had just landed on his back. 'No!' he said. 'Don't even mention that word! If you knew! The troubles, the difficulties!'

Niven had got back some of his fight. He said, 'Look, old Wheelie is back where she began. Mummified, in a tomb! The next time a Humper arrives she'll be *fried*. And then everything will have been for nothing!'

'An Adverse Report!' Banna whispered. 'I could get an Adverse Report! I have five Commendations, the Long Service Star, my Gradings have always been satisfactory ... a lifetime of service, a whole lifetime! And then in *he* comes! Slams open the door, stands there glaring at me –'

'Old Wheelie!' Niven said. 'Never mind Bang-Bang, what about old Wheelie?' Su joined them. She listened, frowning, but said nothing.

'It's different for you two,' Banna piped, 'you are just Cargostrippers, just *boys*. You get a second chance, a third chance ... But me – do you know how old I am?'

'Eighty,' Niven said. 'You told us. About old Wheelie –'

'I am *eighty*!' said Banna, not hearing. 'That is old, you know. When I was a boy, *seventy* was old. You stopped work at sixty-five. And I am eighty, still working – and faced with an Adverse Report ...'

Su said, in her high, light, clear voice, 'Then you are a fool!'

Banna turned to her, his eyes swivelling and popping, his mouth open. 'What did you say? What was that you said?'

'You are a fool,' she repeated. 'You are a slave, a machine, a ... *thing*. And a fool. You've sold yourself *for* nothing, *to* nothing!'

Banna's mouth opened and closed but no words came out.

Noll said, 'But Su! Bang-Bang isn't a nothing, he's Bang-Bang. And if Mr Banna really is going to get an Adverse, it could affect his pension status and –'

Su said, 'You think Bang-Bang is perfect, don't you? All of you. Just because he makes a noise and smacks himself with his splatty little swagger stick! You think he might smack *you*, is that it?'

'Well, come to think of it,' Noll said, 'yes! That's just what Mr Banna thinks! And he could be right!'

Niven said, 'Wait a minute, wait a minute. They're clever, these Chinese. What's going on in your mind, Su?'

'You'd be surprised,' said Su. 'There's a very old Chinese saying. I just made it up. It goes, "When the lion opens his mouth to roar, have a good look down his throat because you never know what you'll find in his belly." Something like that.'

'You've lost me,' said Niven. 'Try again.'

'No, *you* try again,' Su said. 'You make me sick, you three. I don't blame Mr Banna, because –'

'You've been at the *RadRec!*' Banna said, in a whisper. 'You've found out something about the CO! Haven't you? What did you find out?'

'I'm saying nothing. Except that, if I were you three, and I'd done all that work, and some stupid splat with a swagger stick came along, and –'

'You'd go ahead?' Banna asked Su, with his head on one side. He had stopped goggling and twitching.

Su said nothing. Noll said, 'All these hints! ... They don't make *me* feel brave.'

'Eighty!' Banna said, to himself. 'That is old, very

old. Too old to be a machine, a slave, a thing. Isn't that
what you said, Su?'

'Look, I didn't mean –' Su began, but Banna lifted
a thin brown hand.

'Eighty!' he said. 'It is ridiculous! I am an old
man!' He stopped talking to himself and spoke to
Noll and Niven. 'All I care about is this: I want to
start old Wheelie. I want to hear her go, feel her when
she's running. I want a toy for my second childhood!'
He chuckled drily, and walked away from them without looking back.

'Now you've done it!' Niven said, rounding on
Su. 'Now we've got to go ahead – at the worst possible
time, the most dangerous time!'

Noll said, 'I hope you've got something really good
on Bang-Bang, that's all! Have you?'

'Who knows?' Su said. She was frowning, worried.
'I just got tired of you two chickening out ... I didn't
really mean ...'

'Oh, voomy! Fantass! Great!' said Noll disgustedly.

There was silence for a minute until Su said, 'There's
a Humper coming in in five days. I thought you ought
to know.' She wheeled round and walked off.

'A Humper coming in in five days,' Niven repeated
slowly. 'That's all we needed.'

Two days later Banna, Noll and Niven were in the
elephant's trunk, frozen with cold – the trunk was
sealed from the outside air only by flap curtains – and
sweating with fear. But Banna was not sweating.

'I just hope the trunk is light-tight!' Noll complained. 'If Bang-Bang or the cleaners or anyone else
came in, they might see a chink of light from all these
lanterns –'

'Su will warn us,' Banna said and tapped the little PortaComm in his breast pocket. 'Let's get on. It's a clearance of two thou, that doesn't look like two thou. Give me the feeler gauge ...'

'If only the lanterns gave some heat ...,' Niven said. The Rad-powered lanterns threw their cold light on the filthy black cylindrical walls of the trunk and the gleaming black and silver of old Wheelie. 'You're beautiful,' Niven said to old Wheelie. 'And you'll get us all into real trouble, won't you?' The Wheelie, long and low and potent like a resting tiger, replied 'Tink' as Banna put a little spanner to a locking nut. The brown dome on his bald head was slightly blue here and there with the cold.

Niven shrugged and got on with his work: from Wheelie's exhaust pipes there stretched two long, dull rubbery snakes that merged into one, made of Ventrunk – the plastic trunking used for building up ventilator systems. The Ventrunk sections force-fitted together. You rammed one length into another.

Easy work. But it made Niven sweat. Was Banna right? Would Ventrunk really damp the noise of Wheelie's engine? Banna said it would. Noll and Niven thought it might. They did not really want to find out.

Yet the Ventrunk was a clever idea of Banna's. When Banna first suggested it, Noll said, 'You're joking! It isn't just noise, it's fumes. Even if the Ventrunk takes out the noise, the detectors will pick up the fumes, and the alarms will go, and that's it. The detectors will smell us out. That's what they're there for!'

Banna said, 'Yes, yes, the detectors are everywhere. And the air-conditioning reaches everywhere. Very good. Well, where *aren't* there detectors?'

'I don't get you, I don't see what you mean.'

'Look,' said Banna, holding in his impatience. 'The one place in the settlement where there are no detectors is *here*. In the AirCon plant.'

Of course. Wheelie was in the elephant's trunk. The trunk led straight to the air-conditioning plant. The AirCon cleaned air – all air, any air, whether it had triggered the detectors or not. So by using the elephant's trunk as the place to start old Wheelie, you cut out the detectors and went – quietly, odourlessly, safely – straight into the AirCon. Brilliant.

Brilliant, but still nerve-racking. Niven finished his length of Ventrunk and said, 'I'm ready.' Banna and Noll made their way to him, each of them ringed by a halo of lantern light as they moved through the tunnel.

'The tricky bit,' Niven said, pointing at the big inlet grille of the AirCon.

'I don't think so,' said Banna. He prodded uncertainly at the grille. 'There's no warning gear that I can see. No tamperproofing. I mean, who'd want to tamper with the AirCon?'

'We would,' Niven said miserably.

'Then let us tamper,' said Banna. He opened the grille – stuck in the Ventrunk – and held his breath.

Nothing happened. No *wah-wah-wah* siren, no change in the steady hum of the AirCon. The grille simply closed itself steadily, squeezing the Ventrunk almost flat. Banna forced it open and pulled the Ventrunk away. 'A standard adaptor will prevent that,' he said. And fitted one.

They stood for a moment staring at what they had done. Then Noll said shakily, 'I suppose you realize there's nothing to stop us starting her up?'

'Nothing but the noise, and Security people running down here and thumping on the elephant's trunk and shouting for us to come out with our hands up,' Niven said.

'We could at least turn her over,' Noll said. 'See if she *wants* to fire.'

They looked at each other. What seemed a long way down the elephant's trunk was old Wheelie, blazing her chrome and enamel in the light of the lanterns, twinkling like a distant constellation. Hardly knowing it, the three of them walked towards her, watching her twinklings shift and change as they approached.

They were standing by her. She looked very still and long and metallic and somehow expectant.

'We should follow our plan and wait for the Humper,' Niven said. 'It's a good plan. The Humper arrives. Five minutes of solid noise. We start old Wheelie up. Five minutes to get her going and see that she's running O.K., then straight out through the curtain in the Humper bay where we've arranged everything to screen her off. Finally, wheel her back and hide her like we used to.'

'Of course, she might *not* start up,' Noll said. 'Then, if we followed the Humper-day plan, we could be in trouble. She might even be burned up inside the elephant's trunk if the Humper arrived too soon. Without our ever hearing her engine running ...'

'Stick to the plan,' said Niven. He threw a leg over old Wheelie and sat on the saddle, twisting the throttle open a little. 'Wait for the Humper to come,' he said, and pushed the ignition lever to retard. 'Is the petrol tap on?' he said. Banna leaned down and pushed the tap to ON without saying anything.

'Try the compression,' Noll said. 'Just give her a

kick and see how her compression is.' Niven gave her a slow kick and said, 'Boom, boom. No doubt about the compressions!' Old Wheelie gave a little sucking noise.

Banna said, 'Well, everything's in order, then ...' and he silently moved the choke lever. They looked at each other, eyes glinting in the lantern light.

Niven looked at Noll – kicked down strong and hard – and Wheelie coughed, spat and died. 'Well?' he said. 'Shall I?'

Noll nodded, dry-mouthed. Niven put his weight down on the pedal. Wheelie coughed, spat, tinkled and choked. Niven kicked her again. She said, 'HA-HARHAROOMPF!', spat once and then, 'BA-RRRANG! ... BA-RRRANG!' as Niven caught her on the throttle. 'BA-RRRANG!' Wheelie said, deep in her throat: then settled down to a pulsing, chuntering, throbbing beat which smoothed out as Banna eased back the choke lever. You could hear valves and cams busily talking to themselves over the steady hiss of the carburetters.

'Let her run!' said Banna, his face set in a wrinkled mask of pleasure. 'Let her run!'

Niven was astride her with his hands spread wide on the handlebars, laughing. 'She's lovely!' he said. He leaned forward and kissed old Wheelie on the round curve of her headlamp. 'Here,' he said, and gave his seat to Noll. He sat there like an idol with a grinning monkey face. Occasionally he gave her a whiff of throttle: she answered, 'Ba-rrang! ... Ba-rrang!' and then went back to her regular beat.

When Banna took his turn on the saddle, Noll checked the Ventrunk with Niven. 'It's not bad!' he said. And it wasn't. Ten paces from Wheelie, the noise was not all that much. You could feel as much as hear her. Twenty paces away, she was very quiet indeed.

Then her note changed. There were slaps and clicks and once, an ugly metallic clash. Noll gripped Niven's arm. 'He's wrecking her!' he said. 'That moron Banna!' They hurried to him. He looked weirdly thin and small on the big machine. He was grinning to himself and doing things to Wheelie. 'Stop! Stop it!' Noll shouted in his ear, but Banna didn't seem to notice, he went on doing things that made Wheelie judder on her stand and produce clacks and slaps and grunchings.

Niven laughed and said to Noll, 'Look!' The rear wheel was spinning. As they watched, the wheel hesitated, then picked up again, the spokes glinting. It went round at a faster pace. Niven said, 'Don't you see? He's changing gear!'

'So that's what happens!' Noll said, and he watched fascinated as Banna declutched, toed the pedal and set the rear wheel spinning at another speed.

Banna suddenly noticed them and shouted over his shoulder, 'Changing gear! It's good! Fine! Here's second ... third ... fourth! Do you see?'

Noll said, 'It's complicated. I hadn't realized ...' then said, 'I'm going outside to see how much noise she's making. Keep her quiet when I go through the curtains.' Niven saw him walking slowly away, lantern in hand, towards the Humper-bay end of the truck – then running back! 'Cut her!' he shouted, scrabbling at Wheelie's controls.

Banna stopped her and said, very loudly, like a man being woken up, 'What? What?'

'Quiet!' Noll said. 'Not a sound! Lanterns off! My God, I'm lucky! Just as I was going through the curtains, I saw Bang-Bang and his lot, coming this way! Another half-minute and ... Quiet!'

They could hear Bang-Bang now on the other side of the elephant's trunk. His voice sounded tinny and distant, but they knew he was just outside.

'What's he saying?' Niven whispered.

'I can't make it out. Keep quiet!'

'Do you think he knows –'

'Quiet!'

The tinny voice went on. A rumble answered it from time to time. Then the voice receded. 'He's moving on!' Banna muttered. But then came a sound that froze them – CHANG CHANG! – the sound of the elephant's trunk being hit. And then Su's voice, apparently right in their ears, saying, 'Ack my last! Ack my last!'

'How can we acknowledge her last message?' Niven muttered. 'We never heard her first!'

'Why don't you ack?' said Su's voice from the PortaComm. You could tell that she had her mouth right against the mike: tell she was frightened.

'Don't ack her!' Noll said, seeing Banna's hand move to the PortaComm in his pocket. 'If Bang-Bang's on the prowl, they're probably monitoring everything all over the settlement!'

Banna nodded and the three of them crouched in the tunnel. Then – CHANG CHANG! again, only this time very distant. 'It's Bang-Bang's swagger stick,' Noll said, 'that's what it is. I think he's moving away.'

Noll counted to a hundred and said, 'Well. That should be it. He never stays in one place long. Now what?'

'Shouldn't we ack Su? She's taking a risk,' said Niven uneasily.

Banna said, 'You're right. We should.' He spoke into the PortaComm. 'Ack, ack, ack. Stay out. Stay out.' They heard her whisper 'out' and the Porta-Comm stopped hissing.

Niven fingertipped a lantern and a dull glow appeared, enough to show them each other's strained faces. 'It's warm in here,' he said, 'or is it just me being scared?'

Banna said, 'It's warm. That's wrong, it's definitely warm! But that's impossible, the AirCon –'

As he spoke, there was a Whoosh! and they felt cold wind rush past them towards the AirCon.

Noll said, 'We've gone and done it! We stopped the AirCon! Don't you see, that's why it got warm! – we stopped the AirCon!'

'But we couldn't have done!' Banna said, his voice high with fear. 'There was no protection device, no monitor – I looked! –'

'It stopped all the same,' Noll said. 'So we've had it. Bang-Bang must have come down to see what was happening. And he banged on the elephant's trunk just to let us know that he knows about us ...'

'So farewell and goodbye,' said Niven heavily. 'It's goodbye Noll, goodbye Banna, and goodbye Wheelie. Shall we go? After all, we don't want to keep Bang-Bang waiting, do we?'

'Goodbye, Wheelie,' said Noll, and patted the big machine's saddle.

'Goodbye, Wheelie,' said Banna, doing the same.

'Her engine's still warm,' Niven said miserably. 'Oh, well ... At least we started her. Come on, then. Let's go.'

They turned their lanterns on and looked for the last time at Old Wheelie. She glittered fiercely in the light. Banna said, 'Wait!' and went to her: he clicked the petrol tap to OFF.

They walked away from her along the elephant's trunk and prepared to meet their reception committee, headed by Bang-Bang himself.

It took all of five minutes for them to realize that there was no reception committee: that no one wanted to see them: that no one was even interested in them. Nobody talked about the elephant's trunk, or the AirCon or Bang-Bang. Everyone talked of Rad.

Rad had failed for 235 seconds.

The failure left everyone shaken. People were talking about it in hushed whispers instead of getting on with their duties. There were white faces and clumsy movements.

Su's face told them nothing. 'Meet you in the Centre,' she said, and she walked on looking trim and neat but taut.

In the Centre, it was safe to talk because everyone was talking louder than usual. Banna said, 'Niven, don't talk to Su or to me. Let Noll talk to her. We'll split up. I don't want the four of us seen together.'

'O.K.,' said Niven. He joined a group of people of his own age and listened. He learned that the Rad failure had taken place when he was in the elephant's trunk. Most of the settlement's services kept working – the lighting, most of the machines, the Comm – but the AirCon and some others had stopped. 'It's a *big* machine,' a loud girl kept saying. 'Don't you see, it's a big machine, it makes *great* demands on the Rad supply –'

'And we make a big demand on the AirCon,' someone answered her. 'We live or die by it! So stop sounding so smugly reasonable, next time it happens it could be the death of us all!'

'I still don't see why it stopped,' Niven said, wanting to hear opinions – particularly if they were connected with old Wheelie.

The loud girl said, 'Well, that's hardly *surprising*, if you knew *why* it stopped you'd be doing the whole settlement a *big favour*!' She sniffed and turned away from him.

Niven said, 'Any suggestions? Anyone got a theory?'

'Well,' said a RadTech junior, looking wise, 'it's got to be our own module, our own Radball, I mean, it couldn't be a galactic breakdown, that's impossible. So our Radball went on the blink for 235 seconds – sorted itself out – put itself right – and started up again.'

'That's your professional opinion, as a RadTech whizzo?' said the loud girl disgustedly. 'Well, thank you very *much*, I'm sure we've all learned a *lot*!'

'But I don't see,' Niven said politely to the Rad-Tech, 'what would cause our Radball to break down. I mean, has anything unusual happened on the settlement?'

'Well, of course, there's a continuing feedback of settlement environmental factors to the Radball,' the RadTech man began.

The loud girl said, 'Splat!' and he shut up.

'But *has* anything happened on the settlement?' Niven repeated. 'Anything at all unusual? I mean, Bang-Bang's inspection wasn't to do with anything unusual?' Niven insisted. But nobody had anything to say.

'So old Wheelie's safe!' Niven said to himself: and

bought a Maltchoc Whip to celebrate.

A few tables farther along the Centre, Su said, 'It can't have been anything to do with you-know-what. It just *can't* have been!'

'But it's a bit spooky, isn't it?' Noll said. 'Why should the Radball go ape just at the very time we were with old –'

'Coincidence. Nothing but coincidence. Just the same coincidence that made Noll leave the elephant's trunk when Bang-Bang arrived!' She shuddered.

'What *was* Bang-Bang doing? Why was he inspecting? What was he looking for?'

'Look,' Su said impatiently, 'there's nothing in that either. He had an inspection because he wanted to have an inspection. He tapped his splatty cane on the elephant's trunk because he felt like it. And Rad broke down just then because it felt like it. The breakdown couldn't have happened at a better time for you and old Wheelie!'

'But it's funny that the Rad breakdown should have happened just when we were starting up old Wheelie. And anyhow, you were supposed to Comm us and warn us if anything went wrong –'

'I did, you moron, I did!' Su said, rolling her eyes with disgust. 'But you didn't answer because you were *making a noise*, remember? A very special sort of noise!'

'I suppose so,' said Noll. 'But it's funny that the Rad –'

Su said, 'I can't stand another moment of this!'

Noll said, 'Sorry! I'm sorry! It's just that it was so strange in that trunk ... and *she* was so voomy ... I wish you'd been there, Su!'

'Now you're talking!' she said. 'Tell me about her again. But keep your voice down ...'

So he told her again about old Wheelie; and didn't tell her again about the feeling he had that, somehow, starting up old Wheelie had stopped the Radball on Terramare 3. Because, as Su said, there couldn't be any connection.

Life on the settlement kept changing. For the worse.

Banna got older by the minute. Su said, 'Poor man, he's down again. He's getting the splatty end of the Bang-Bang purity drive. I mean, Banna is Controller of Personnel, so he gets all the bull.'

They watched Banna sit down at a table filled with his own staff. When he sat, he seemed to have lost his neck: his head sat inside his narrow shoulders.

'You'd have thought Bang-Bang had more important things on his mind,' Niven said. 'Rad, for instance. The Rad blackout. That really *was* important.'

'Ah,' said Su, '*Aaah!*'

'What do you mean, *ah?*'

'Nothing. Just *ah*.'

Niven gave a snort and said to Noll, 'It's catching, the atmosphere in this splatty place! Now Su's caught it. Being the oriental mystery woman, are you, Su?'

Su hissed, 'Quietly! Don't shout!'

Noll said, 'There's no need to be rude!'

'Well, she makes me sick.'

Su said, 'All right, but be quiet!'

'Look,' Niven said, 'I'll stand on the table and yell if I feel like it! I'll shout "Su fancies Bang-Bang!" – any crazy thing I choose.'

He had talked himself into a temper. 'All this mystery stuff,' he grumbled, 'just because you work in

51

RadRec and think you *know* something ...'

They ate silently and sulkily. The Centre was very quiet. If you listened carefully, you could pick out one word from the conversations. The word was Rad.

The Comm crackled. There was a string of announcements about inspections, report there, do this, that and the other. 'Come on,' said Noll. 'Let's get the hell out and go and hide ourselves somewhere!'

Niven said, 'I'm sick of all this bull and Bang-Bang. I'm going to look at Wheelie. Sit astride her. Muck about with her controls.'

Noll said, 'Don't! That's stupid! You know the plan! Leave her alone until the Humper lands! Stick to the plan! Tell him, Su, tell him he's being stupid!'

'You're being stupid,' Su told Niven coldly.

'I'm going all the same,' Niven announced, and walked out on them.

Inside the elephant's trunk, it was lonely. Niven began to have regrets. It was very cold, colder than last time. He had brought only two lanterns and their blue-ish light depressed him. They didn't show the Wheelie to best advantage either. She looked dead and cold. Just metal.

'But you're not, are you?' Niven said, running his hands over the gold emblem on her tank. 'You're a wonderful old girl, aren't you?' He looked at her, wondering why they had ever called Wheelie 'her'. The Wheelie wasn't her, it was a him.

Even sitting astride the Wheelie, it was dead, dark, cold and lonely inside the elephant's trunk. There was blackness behind him, blackness in front of him and a ring of cold, dirty light around him, 'Fear of enclosed spaces,' Niven said to himself. 'What's the word for that?' He thought for a moment and said, 'Oh yes. Claustrophobia.'

He turned on the ignition. The little warning light Banna had installed lit up. It gleamed yellow.

'Yellow,' Niven muttered to himself. 'Very appropriate! Your colour, yellow. You're scared of everything, aren't you, lad? Fear of enclosed spaces, fear of being a cargohumper all your life, fear of old Wheelie being discovered. So here you are, scared rotten, talking to an old motorbike. Not starting it, not running it, not riding it, oh no! Just hiding somewhere dark and talking to it. No guts!'

He kicked Wheelie's starter again. Nothing. 'Splat!' he shouted, and opened taps, pulled and thumbed levers, twisted a grip, kicked again. Nothing.

'You ... stupid ... old ...' he yelled, giving her a kick with each word. And she started.

BA-RRANG! He gave her more throttle, less choke. BA-BA-RRRANG! 'No guts, eh?' Niven shouted, above the din – caught her stuttering motor on the throttle, smoothed out her roars and sat back, arms straight, making himself keep calm. Mustn't race her. Let the oil warm up and circulate. Even at a fast idle, he could feel her power, feel her loosening her muscles and settling down. Getting ready for business.

He switched on the lights. First a yellowish glow patterned with the lines moulded in the headlamp glass, then full beam! – a white cone pushing right down the elephant's trunk all the way to the curtains. He squeezed the clutch lever and felt with his foot for the gearchange. What was it you had to do for first? Down or up? It didn't matter, she was still on her stand, he couldn't hurt her even if he did it wrong.

Grrunch! – and then the whirr of chains as the engine drove the gearbox and the final drive reached the rear wheel!

He put both feet on the ground and pushed forward against the bars. She didn't move. He tried again and she rocked up over the stand a little and settled back. He gave her a hard push, using all his strength jerkily. The throttle twisted open and Wheelie roared and bellowed – even the Ventrunk couldn't absorb the noise – and then she tipped forward over the stand and her handlebars swung and pulled the clutch lever out of his hand –

Wheelie's spinning rear tyre yelped as it hit ground. She jumped forward, bellowing, twisting herself away from Niven's hands. She left him on his hands and knees then fell down SLAM on her side, with her handlebars skewed round and her headlamp burning a white oval on the ceiling of the elephant's trunk. She had pulled her exhausts clear of the Ventrunk and the noise was deafening.

Niven picked himself up, leapt at Wheelie, cut switches, turned off her petrol tap. The engine died. He ran a shaking hand over the downward flank of her tank – it was all right, the tank was dry, she wasn't spilling petrol. He'd done everything that needed to be done, all that was left was to get her back on her stand, double-check everything, look for damage and switch off the headlamp. But he was still shaking.

He pulled her upright. She weighed a ton. It took him a minute of heaving and straining before he could get her up. When she *was* up, he was afraid she would topple over on him but she didn't. Groaning with the effort and the worry of dropping her, he managed at last to rock her back on her stand. She stood on the curved floor of the elephant's trunk, slightly to one side and not quite upright, but safe again. Her head-lamp beam made a white slash against the curved wall of the trunk.

Still panting and cursing, he looked her over. Not a trace, hardly a scratch – just a bright scrape-mark where the clutch lever had scraped the floor of the elephant's trunk.

He inspected her sides, her exhausts and pedals. Nothing there either. He couldn't see properly so he reached for a lantern. The lantern was out! So he groped for the other. But that was out too.

He said, 'Stupid, splatty lanterns, what's the use of –' Then stopped, frozen by a chill under his layer of sweat. The lanterns were out: but Rad lanterns can't, don't, will not go out.

Not unless Rad goes out.

He stood, frozen, staring at the lantern in his hand. He put the lantern under the beam of Wheelie's head-lamp. All he saw was a Rad lantern with the sensor in the ON position. The other lantern was the same. They were ON and they were not working.

He murmured, 'AirCon!' and listened. The AirCon was working. But then, it *would* work. After the first scare, Bang-Bang had had its standby checked and re-checked.

Niven shuddered. He picked up the two useless lanterns, turned off Wheelie's lights and made for the curtains at the end of the elephant's trunk. He had to walk slowly. He had plenty of time to tell himself the things he thought he needed telling. 'You gutless wonder!' he began, groping his way along the tunnel, 'You've told the whole settlement about Wheelie. You've shouted, "Look! here it is!" in everyone's ear. You've behaved like a kid – proved you can't begin to manage Wheelie – and given yourself hysterics. Is there anything more you need to know about yourself? Is there anything else you've done?'

Just before he reached the curtains, he got his answer. There was a low note that rose, then got higher, then rose and fell.

'Wah – wah – wah!' went the sirens. 'Wah – wah – wah – wah!'

Niven was filthy, but nobody noticed. The emergency lights were on, the settlement was dark and everyone was in a hurry. He went to the washroom and cleaned himself up, then reported for duty.

He should have been given a rocket by his section commander for reporting late but he wasn't. The SecCo simply said, 'You're not needed here, go to the Centre.'

He went to the Centre. Nearly everyone was there and Bang-Bang was on the stage, walking back and forth. He was twitching his swagger stick against the back of his knees as he walked. The Centre looked dim with only the emergency lights on and it was very quiet. People just stood waiting, expressionless.

More people came in. SecCos went to Bang-Bang and made their reports, too quietly to be overheard. A group of five CommCentre staff arrived and one of them, a woman, said, 'All present, sir. No casualties to report.'

Bang-Bang said, 'CommSec?'

The CommSec woman said, 'We reported to Earthside, sir, and told them our situation.'

'What do they say?'

'We're to do our best, sir.'

Bang-Bang said, 'All right. Do our best. Whatever that may mean. Right. You know the situation. We have had another Rad failure and are running the AirCon and other services on emergency supplies. That means forty-eight hours. Is that correct?'

A Rad-Rec senior said, 'Forty to forty-eight hours, sir.'

Bang-Bang said, 'No Rad, no air or anything else after forty to forty-eight hours. So please eat and speak and breathe sparingly. If you find yourself with nothing to do, do nothing: go to sleep. Don't waste energy, don't argue, don't fool about. *Conserve air.* Understood? Right. Any more questions?'

He smacked himself with his swagger stick, pretending to be impatient. But the question he did not want asked was asked. A head bobbed up and an unsteady voice shouted, 'Look, we're all going to die, aren't we? We're all going to die ...!'

Bang-Bang said, 'Yes. That is an essential condition of human existence.' Someone laughed, then others; then there was a brief rattle of applause.

The man who had asked the question said, 'Oh, my God!' and someone answered him with a gruff, 'Belt up!'

Another voice said, 'I'm a RadTech, sir. Is there nothing useful we can do – about the Radball, I mean? Can't we do *anything*?'

Bang-Bang said, 'The Radball is sited on the other side of Terramare 3. If it were sited where it should be, near this settlement, we could recode it. As it isn't, we can't. As a member of RadTech section, you should know that.'

Still another voice, hollow with fear, asked, 'But can't we reach the Radball somehow? Can't we? I know it's three hundred kilometres away, but *surely* –'

Bang-Bang went *whack* with his swagger cane against his thigh and said, 'How do you propose to reach the Radball? By putting on a suit and walking there? That would take too long. With our vehicles? But our vehicles are all Rad-powered. To reach the Radball, we need Rad. There is an old saying, "If we had some ham, we could have ham and eggs – *if we had some eggs*".'

Noll said in Su's ear, 'Well, at least we can say we've had our chips!' She did not smile.

'Any more questions?' said Bang-Bang. 'No? Then report here again at 0900. Those who can, sleep. Those who can't – enjoy yourselves. Preferably without breathing.'

He gave an abrupt smile and left.

A pretty girl next to Niven said, 'Well ... So this is what dying is like!' and started laughing jerkily. Niven stared at her and chewed his thumbnail.

Life on the settlement slid into new gears. You could see the new situation taking different people in different ways. 'Sleep!' Bang-Bang had said – and some took to their beds straightaway and lay there, eyes open, staring at nothing and seeing their own deaths, stage by stage.

Others talked endlessly. They went on and on and on about their Earthside memories, why they should never have come to the settlement, how unfair everything was, who was to blame for the mess, how it need never have happened if only ...

Some people became suddenly conscientious. They went about their duties with a new energy, tidying files, checking circuits, turning out their quarters, cleaning behind things that had never before been cleaned behind. An old boy from the kitchens was cleaning behind and around the table where Noll, Niven, Su and Banna sat. He was hissing between his teeth as he rubbed and polished. Sometimes he said, 'Oh dear, oh-dear-oh-dear!' in a sort of moan, then went on polishing.

At last Niven said, 'Enough! Go and do whatever you're doing somewhere else!' and the cleaner shuffled off.

'What are *we* going to do?' Su said. She was one of the calm ones. Her face showed nothing. But Banna never stopped rubbing and massaging his face.

Noll said, 'Mr Banna! Did the Wheelie cause the Rad breakdown?'

Banna said, 'It was not a "breakdown", the Radball merely did what it is programmed to do. Oh, that damnable machine of yours! If only –'

Niven said, 'But what did the Wheelie *do*, Mr Banna?'

'It produced electrical emissions,' Banna said wearily. 'It put out frequencies, voltages, currents – all of them unfamiliar to the Radball's detectors and protectors. No doubt the Radball picked them up, analysed them, classified them as "pirates" – and stopped, until the appropriate action could be taken. But it can't be taken. And here we are in this hopeless situation –'

'What must be done to get Rad going again, Mr Banna?'

'Get to the Radball, recode it. Which we can't do. "If we had some ham, *if* we had some eggs ..."'

'Well, can't you think of an answer? I can,' Niven said. 'Can't you?'

Su had been listening to the whispered words. She said, 'Wheelie?'

'Wheelie ...!' Noll murmured. 'Of course! She's the only thing that can move long distances under her own power! She's the only way of reaching the Radball!'

Banna said, 'Eighty. Eighty! If I were starting again – if I were young, like you three –'

Niven said, 'I vote we go to Bang-Bang and lay it on the line for him. Noll?'

Noll said, 'But we can't! You know what he's like! He'd just clap us in irons, throw us into a dungeon – or whatever it is they did in his time!'

Su said, 'Look at Banna. Look at all the other faces. They think they're going to die. We could stop it. Couldn't we?'

Noll said, 'But Bang-Bang wouldn't listen, he wouldn't want Terramare saved our way. And besides, how do we know we could do it?'

Su said, 'How do you know we can't do it?'

Niven said, 'How much petrol is there, Banna?'

'Petrol? What does it matter now? There is plenty of petrol. Why do you talk about petrol?'

Niven said, 'Come on then, you two. We're off to see old Bang-Bang and tell him the facts of life.'

Su said, 'I've got one fact of his life that may come in handy ...'

They went to see the Commanding Officer.

He wasn't in his office. Ever since the emergency, he had made himself stride – but not too fast – round the settlement. 'Keep up morale,' he told his assistants.

'There he is!' Noll said. The man was standing rigidly by a group of RadTechs, smacking his thigh with his swagger stick and making light conversation. As he talked, he kept breaking his face into jerky little smiles.

'Excuse me, sir,' Niven said.

Bang-Bang said, 'One moment,' and went on talking to the RadTechs.

'Excuse me, sir. It's urgent.'

'No doubt. But wait.' More light conversation with the RadTechs: then Bang-Bang turned to Niven and said, 'What do you want? Stand straight, don't slouch.'

'Talk in your office, sir, if you don't mind,' Niven said.

Su said, 'It's very important!' and Bang-Bang glared at her.

Then he smacked himself with his stick and said, 'Very well,' and led them to his office. He plunged into his big chair and said, 'What is it?'

They told him about Wheelie. When Niven dried up, Noll took over. The man's face never showed surprise, never changed its expression.

When they had finished, he said, 'Right. I'll summarize. Motor-bicycle and fuel, correct? No dependency on Rad, correct? So you can ride to the Radball, recode it and save the settlement, correct?'

'Yes sir,'

'And you expect me to support you – to authorize you to go?'

'Yes sir.'

'You expect me to condone a criminal offence – several criminal offences, defying the Oil Ban, illegal possession of a petrol-engined vehicle, misuse of Galaxy transport, smuggling, defiance of every other Regulation in the book –'

Su spoke for the first time. Her voice was shaky. 'It's too late to accuse us, too late ... Which comes first? The Regulations, or the lives of all the people on this settlement?'

He said, 'You address me as sir!' and began tapping the edge of the desk with his stick. 'And do not attempt to tell me how to apply the Regulations: I know.'

She said, 'But the Regulations won't *help*, they won't *do* anything useful. Surely you see that?' Bang-Bang just tapped with his stick.

Su's face and voice hardened. 'The settlement was installed thirteen years ago,' she said. 'Isn't that right? Sir?'

'I fail to see what the inauguration date has to do with the present situation,' Bang-Bang said. The cane went tap, tap, tap, still faster.

'The Regulations,' Su insisted, 'the Regulations haven't changed in thirteen years, I think ... ?'

Noll glanced at Niven. They shrugged at each other, not understanding.

'Thirteen years ago,' Su began – but Bang-Bang brought his cane down SLAP on the table and said, 'Show me the motor-bicycle!'

As they walked to the elephant trunk and Wheelie, Niven muttered, 'What was all that about? What was she on about?' Noll pulled a don't-know face.

They got Wheelie out of the elephant trunk: wheeled her in. She stood by the Humper bay and glittered darkly and powerfully at them. Noll wiped elephant-trunk dust from her saddle and tank. 'There she is,' he said. 'Sir,' he added, absent-mindedly.

Bang-Bang walked round her; stood in front of her with his legs apart; and said, 'Start her.'

Noll and Niven methodically went through the Open, On, Prime, Choke, Ignition, Throttle drill. Then Noll straddled her and kicked down on the starter.

Wheelie roared. BA-RRRANG! she bellowed, spitting petrol smells from her exhausts. The din boomed and echoed round the Humper bay. Then she settled down to her pattern of distant thunder, glop-glop and tinkle, whirr and throb. Noll beamed at Niven, and Niven beaming back wiped her mudguards tenderly with the cleaning rag.

Bang-Bang said, 'So. Time for decisions.'

Su reached across Niven, seized the throttle handgrip and twisted it. Wheelie yelled BA-RRRANG! and shot little plumes of thin smoke.

'The whole settlement heard your decision, sir,' Su said.

Bang-Bang spoke into his PortaComm. 'RadTech, report Humper bay.' In seconds, five RadTechs came running. They saw Wheelie and gaped.

'You were ordered to conserve air!' Bang-Bang remarked. 'Don't *run*.' The RadTechs did not seem to hear him: they goggled at Wheelie. Two of them began to smile, sillily.

Bang-Bang said, 'Ecosuits. How many?'

Noll said, 'Two. One each.'

Bang-Bang said, 'Right. One for me, one for one or other of you.'

'One for you?' Noll said. 'You must be joking! She's ours! Wheelie's ours! no one is going to ride her but us!'

'I have experience of these machines,' Bang-Bang said loftily. He walked towards Wheelie.

'Perhaps you know the carburetter settings for the air outside, sir?' Noll said. 'You know just which adjustments to make? You've spent hours working out the pressure and temperature factors?'

Bang-Bang made no reply.

'We ride her,' Niven said, grasping the handlebars more firmly. 'Us or nobody. Nobody but us!'

Su said, 'They ride her, sir.'

Bang-Bang gave her what Noll and Niven thought was an uneasy sideways glance: then with a short barking laugh, he said, 'Well. Right. Where are the Ecosuits?'

Two RadTechs fetched the gleaming silver Ecosuits and 'goldfish bowls' – the helmets. Silently, Noll and Niven stripped themselves of their working clothes and put on the real-wool inners, with spiderweb heating wires woven into the wool fibres; then the 'silks', the outers; then the goldfish bowls, They cut Wheelie's motor and stood still, with arms and legs spread, while the RadTechs went through the familiar checkouts. BaseComm, InterComm, AirCon, Mobility Check, Pressure Equalization, Full Inflation/No Inflation, Reserve and Fallback Supplies, Demist, Nutrition, Excretion, MayDay Voluntary, Mayday Auto, MendPak, AirPak, MediPak ... The Ecosuits had carried humans through a hundred environments in light-years of galactic travel. They were good suits, familiar suits.

The checkout took five minutes. At the end of it, a RadTech's voice in Noll's and Niven's ears said, 'O.K. Try sitting on the machine.'

They sat on the Wheelie, Noll in front. Everything seemed fine. Noll said, 'Niven, pretend I'm braking hard. What happens if you jerk forward? Try it.' Their helmets clashed. The RadTechs fitted buffers to the front and backs of the goldfish bowls.

'O.K.?'

'O.K.'

A RadComm girl came in with six Plastix. Bang-Bang took the little cards, slipped three into each of Noll's and Niven's Ecosuits. 'Your instructions,' he said to Noll and Niven. 'Play them.' Noll and Niven each put a gloved hand over the pockets. Circuits linked, the Plastix spoke their message into their ears: 'Proceed to Radball, following bleepcode routing. On reaching destination recode Radball. Recode by opening the trap marked CODE and inserting any of your Plastix in the slot above and to the left of the trap. When the recode is effective, the sign by the slot will light up and read EFFECTIVE. If the first recode is not effective, try the second and third recodes. You have six recode sequences in all. This signal authorized by ...'

The Plastix read off a string of gobbledygook and Noll and Niven took their hands from over their pockets.

'Clear?' said Bang-Bang.

'Yes,' Noll replied. 'Why six recode sequences, though? Why not just one?'

'Safety in numbers,' said Bang-Bang. 'Whatever circumstances caused the Radball to stop, we want a recode sequence that will make it start. RadComm have worked out six sequences. Understood?'

'O.K.'

RadTech men had been checking over old Wheelie. The uncertain voice of one of them said, 'Sir ... We've checked the machine, nothing to report. Spare petrol in six separate containers, spare oil in two. Sir, there's a question about tyre pressures, these pneumatic tyres –'

Noll interrupted. 'No worry about that. The tyres are solid extrusions, not air-filled.'

Bang-Bang said, 'They are, are they? And where were they made? When? By whom?' Then he checked himself and said, 'Never mind. Get on. Anything else?'

· Noll said, 'Helmets clear, sir.' The suits were tuning themselves in. When the goldfish bowls cleared, you knew you were ready to go. Already the suits were emitting human steam in the cold air of the Humper bay. The goldfish bowls were clearing their last traces of breath, the warmed air was circulating. Niven turned down his temperature, he didn't want to waste the PowerPak – without Rad, they had to depend on the P Ps.

'Anything else?' Bang-Bang said again.

'No sir,' said Noll and Niven.

'Then here is my final message, which is being recorded,' Bang-Bang said. His voice was cold. 'You are volunteers. You are acting of your own free will, though under my authority. Agreed?'

'Agreed.'

. 'If your mission fails, for any reason whatsoever, we cannot sustain you or mount a rescue operation. Is that understood?'

'Understood.'

'Then that is all. You may go.'

Su's voice cut across. 'Noll! Niven! Good luck!'

They smiled at her. Niven waved. Noll kicked the starter. Wheelie fired instantly. Noll kept her running at a fast tickover, pulled in full clutch and dabbed with his toe at the gear lever. His foot felt strange: the suit. He tried again, and felt first gear notch in. 'Watch it, now!' he muttered to Niven, and relaxed his clutch hand, fraction by fraction. The travel in the lever seemed to go on for ever –

Then he felt the clutch begin to bite, and Wheelie moved. She inched forward uncertainly while Noll's hand, a rigid claw, kept the clutch lever in just that certain place. He gave her a bit more throttle and she moved more.

Then she was actually going! – bumbling across the floor of the Humper bay, kept upright by Noll's feet and sometimes Niven's. Noll gave her more throttle. Wheelie lurched to the left – she felt heavy and threatening, not like the soft little Moppet he was used to – but he let her run in a big circle, they both had their feet up now. 'Second gear?' he shouted and Niven replied, 'You're doing fine ... fine!'

They went right round the Humper bay and Noll brought in second. It went in quite easily but threw Wheelie forward with a lurch of power that turned into a near-stall as the clutch went home and the revs died. Noll gave her a bit more throttle and made another circuit. He was getting the hang of it. Niven's voice said, 'Fine ... fine!' in his ear.

Noll said, 'One more time round and then we're out. Open the doors. O.K.?'

Bang-Bang's voice said, 'Doors open. Both doors. You can go straight through.'

Noll answered, 'Thank you, sir.' And meant it. Regulations did not allow both doors to be opened at once, it wasted settlement air and let in the freezing cold, hostile gases of Terramare 3's atmosphere. So Bang-Bang was ignoring the Regs – and he was saving Noll from having to stop Wheelie in the airlock between the two doors and start her again to let her through the second door.

He made his third circuit and saw a widening view of the flat cold light of Terramare 3 ahead of him as the doors opened. He headed for the gap – it was big now, the doors were fully open – and headed out, giving Wheelie a touch more throttle to steady his steering.

They were through. Niven looked back. He caught a last group of the settlement people, with the stiff figure of Bang-Bang in the centre, and the RadTechs and the others bending forward as the Terramare cold bit into them – and Su running after them, one arm waving, her mouth open and shouting something. Then she too had to give in to the cold, she clasped herself and her mouth made a black O. Already the doors were closing: that was the last he saw of her, a hunched figure locked into itself with cold. But her eyes still followed Niven, and were on him as the big doors sliced shut, cutting him off from her, and the settlement, and breathable air, and the polished tables in the Centre. Cutting him off from everything.

Noll said, 'I'm going into third gear!' His voice was cheerful and excited. There was a judder and Wheelie's engine lowered its voice. They were in third, and gaining speed.

'Voomy!' Noll shouted. Niven said nothing. He just clung on as Wheelie, enjoying herself now, made faint tyre marks in the ice-and-sand surface of Terramare 3.

An hour later, Wheelie's speedo showed that she had covered 43 miles without missing a beat. 'We'll stop!' Noll said, and applied the brakes, very gently. Wheelie squeaked a lining, made a sharp 'fizz' as her rear wheel skidded but then obeyed Noll and, half a mile later, stopped. Noll cut the engine. Dead silence, except for the bleeps in their helmets, telling them they were on course.

'We'll change over,' Noll said, in a quiet, remote voice. They did not get off Wheelie. She began to make ticking noises as the cold chilled her warm metal. They sat astride her, listening to the clicks and looking at the landscape.

It was hardly a landscape: just a sheet meeting another sheet. The sheet they rested on was ice, dull sand-ice, ice unbroken by hills or rocks or vegetation. The sheet above them was the sky, a dull sky evenly lit by two suns. Where the two sheets met there was a curve, the horizon. You could only just see it, the colours of the two sheets were so much alike. But if you looked, the curve became plain. It was a sharp curve because Terramare 3 was a very small planet.

Niven got off Wheelie and walked about, glad to move his arms and legs. There was nothing else to see so he looked at Noll, a crystal-headed silver insect astride a strange, old-fashioned, black and silver machine. 'You know what we forgot?' he called to Noll. 'We forgot a camera! You look really weird sitting there ... you, and Wheelie, and two shadows, and nothing else! Voomy!'

Noll said, 'I'm surprised they got your goldfish bowl on over your ears. Very surprised.' The silver globe-headed insect that was Niven made a rude sign. Then he patted Wheelie's tank. She clicked away to herself and dropped a single brown spot of oil on the iced sand.

'I'm eating,' Noll told Niven.

'Me too. I'm hungry. It's all been so ... weird.' He couldn't think of anything else to say and sucked away at the tubes, soup first, then a mouthful of cereal, then more soup.

'We've never been this far from the settlement before,' Noll said. 'We're what old Jut-Jaw Johnson said we'd be: pioneers!'

They went on eating. 'I'm checking my suit,' Niven said. 'All O.K. You?'

'All O.K. You can take over now, whenever you're ready.' His voice was uncertain.

'Fine,' Niven said. 'Shall I take her solo first?'

'No. I don't think so. The extra weight gives her more bite on the ice, I suppose. I'm just checking her levels, she seems O.K.' After a pause, he said, 'Niven, what's the opposite of claustrophobia?'

'Fear of confined spaces? The opposite? I don't know.'

'Agoraphobia! That's it! Dislike of wide open spaces, agoraphobia.'

'So what?'

'So I've got it. What a splatty planet this is.'

'Yup. Well, don't think about it. I'm not thinking about it.'

There was silence for a minute while Niven completed his check of Wheelie, then Noll said, 'Right. Ready to go. You'll take it easy, won't you? Till you're used to her?'

'Of course I will! What do you mean –'

'Nothing, just take it easy.'

Niven started her and, frowning, carefully declutched, selected first and began to let in the clutch. Behind him, Noll said, 'Easy, now!'

Niven felt the clutch begin to bite and spread his fingers a little wider –

Wheelie's rear wheel fizzed and they found themselves lying on the ice. Niven threw himself clear: Noll was pinned by the Wheelie. They pushed and pulled at her, somehow got Noll clear, somehow got Wheelie upright.

Noll hopped around on one leg, holding the other. Niven caught hold of him and said, 'Quieten down, quieten down! Let me look!' He looked at Noll's leg. There was a black mark where a part of Wheelie had burned into the fabric of the Ecosuit. 'It's all *right*, it's not *leaking*, leave it *alone*!' Noll yelled, but Niven got a MendPak from his thigh pocket and applied a patch.

Silently, Niven started Wheelie. 'Hop on,' he said.

Noll said, 'Oh, no! I'll drive, thank you!'

'You won't, you know!'

'Look, after that display of how-not-to-do-it just now, I'd rather –'

'I'm in front. You're behind. Get on.'

Noll got on. Niven started the engine. Once again, he went through the routine of engaging first, declutching, letting in the clutch tenderly, carefully, slowly ...

Wheelie oozed off and away as gently as oil running down the inside of a jar.

'A hundred miles up!' Noll shouted. He was driving again. Niven's drive had been perfect. Smooth, fast and fifty miles put into the hour, nearly all in top gear. They had changed seats at 86 miles. The total distance to the Radball was 172 miles and they had agreed to split the mileage into four.

'How's she feeling?' Niven said.

'Wheelie? Great. Voomy. Ooops!' They hit a hump,

then a series of frozen ripples. The Wheelie soaked them up, liking them. But the ground was changing: the billards-table smoothness was finished, there were patches of ripple and some shallow steps here and there where the sand-and-ice sheet had broken and mended. Once, there had even been a hill that had brought Wheelie down to third gear. Twice, they had seen vegetation: clumpy, seaweedy, low-growing, fleshy plants, grey-green-white. Plants that looked like survivors, not conquerors.

The bleeps sounding in their helmets kept them on course. It was like a game. If you heard nothing – just a low, soothing whistle – you were on course. As soon as you strayed, the note rose and broke into code. The higher the note, the greater your difference from your proper course. *B-b-beep* meant 'you are left of course', *Beepy-beepy-beepy*' meant 'right'. The course beeps came from the settlement. So did messages, every half hour. They were always the same, 'Anything to report?' 'Nothing to report.' 'Repeat, anything to report?' 'Repeat, nothing to report.' 'O.K. and out.' 'O.K. and out.' There was no call-sign, none was needed. No statement of progress, the settlement computed that. Just the deliberately cold, clear, impersonal voice.

The bumps got worse. Noll enjoyed them. It gave him a chance to come to terms with Wheelie, to understand her. A Moppet soaked up anything, the Wheelie had to be driven. A Moppet had no power, the Wheelie was all power – and the power could be your undoing. A Moppet was just a sponge on two fat wheels, the Wheelie an acrobatic prizefighter.

Niven said, 'Hey, steady. You'll have me off!' Noll angled Wheelie into a particularly nasty flurry of ripples and steps and said, 'Sorry.' He was sorry, but not very, for Niven sitting behind him. Wheelie lurched – Noll gave her some throttle – she corrected herself, dug in, rocketed forward. Nice, very nice. He toed-in top gear and said, 'You hardly need touch the clutch. Did you know that?'

'I'm hardly touching the saddle!' Niven complained. 'Slow down!'

When they saw the Radball, only one sun was still in the sky. It shone low and behind the sphere. The effect was dramatic but not what they had expected. Earthside Radballs were clean and shiny things, standing above ground. This one showed a dirty dome, red-purple in the suns' low light.

With Wheelie slowed to a crawl, they circled the Radball. Niven said, 'Hell! It's sunk! We'll have to dig down to get to the bit we want!' They stopped Wheelie, put her on her stand and left her to click to herself while they inspected the Radball.

'You're right. We'll have to dig down, through the ice. But we haven't got a spade, we haven't got anything!'

Noll began to dig at the ice with his hands. The ground was like slippery rock. Niven said, 'Don't do that, your gloves won't take it!'

Noll stopped. 'What do we do, then?'

Niven said, 'We've got the Wheelie. Suppose we started her up and pointed her exhausts at the ground ... What do you think?'

Noll shrugged and said, 'Well ...'

They tried it. After a long time, they had made a dip in the ice about six inches deep. 'No good,' said Niven.

The settlement voice came on. 'Anything to report?'

'We are at the Radball, and –'

'We know that. Anything to report?'

'It's sunk down in the ice! Now what are we supposed to do?'

'Stand by.' Click, and silence.

The remaining sun was rising higher, casting a mean, unwelcoming light on the dome of the Radball. Niven shivered inside his suit, but not from cold. He said, 'I'm going to eat again. Fuel up.' He began sucking his tubes but the food and drink tasted of the settlement, and the Centre, and familiar things. Not of this place.

Click! Bang-Bang's voice. 'How much fuel have you used to reach the Radball?'

'The gauge shows gallons. Say four or five gallons.'

'Very well, we will talk in miles and gallons. You have done 175 miles and have used possibly five gallons. Is that correct?'

'Yes, that could be about it.'

'So you will use the same amount of fuel to get back. Which means that you have a surplus of fuel, correct?'

'Yes. Plenty. More than we need.'

Banna's high, scratchy voice came in. 'Niven?'

'Yes. Hallo, Mr Banna! It's nice to hear a human voice for a change!'

'Many congratulations! Are you all right? Is the machine all right? How fortunate that we didn't fit the Rad ignition! What a good thing you insisted on keeping everything "original"!'

Someone in the background told Banna not to waste

words. Noll said, 'Everything's all right – but the Rad-ball's not, it's buried –'

'Listen, Noll, I think I have an answer,' said Banna. His voice sounded twenty years younger. 'The trap in the Radball is quite high up ... You see, Earthside, to prevent tampering, they mounted the trap quite high, out of reach –'

The background voice snarled again. Niven said, 'If that's Bang-Bang, tell him to –'

Noll said, 'Shut up, Niven. Go on, Banna.'

Banna said, 'Fill the petrol tank with fuel. Fill it right up. Use your empty fuel containers. Only the metal ones, not the others. Crush them into the shape of bowls. Pour fuel into them and set light to it. The containers should sink through the ice. O.K.?'

'O.K. Very voomy. We'll try it.'

They filled Wheelie and jumped on the empty fuel cans; filled them with petrol; and set fire to the first one. The flame went *whoosh*! 'The heat's being wasted,' Niven said. He put another crushed container on top to hold in the heat.

Noll said, 'We shouldn't have jumped on those cans. Look!' He showed Niven the sole of his Ecosuit. There was a cut in it but it didn't go right through.

Niven said, 'Just a tiny bit deeper, and we'd be playing games with the MendPaks. Tricky games ...' He looked worried for a moment but then went back to the fire. The non-metal containers burned too, they discovered. As they burned, they formed a sickly, sticky black mess and let off dirty black smoke. The smoke rose straight into the freezing air, then flattened out into a straight line. Terramare 3 had a thin layer of atmosphere.

The fire was doing its job. 'Banna, we can see it!' Noll reported. 'We can see the top of the trap!' They threw on another splash of petrol. *Whoosh!*

The battered cans had disappeared. They had sunk in the ice and the little trap marked CODE could be opened.

'You do it, Noll,' Niven said. 'Go on. Historic moment!'

'Toss you for it.' They tossed one of Wheelie's spanners. It came down showing the unmarked side. 'I win,' said Noll. He opened the hatch, found the slot for the coding card and put in one of the six Plastix. It went in the slot like a visiting card. The Radball digested it and made some noises, little clicks and ticks. Nothing else happened.

They fed in the second card and the Radball chittered to itself. But that was all. Noll and Niven looked at each other. Niven said, 'Here, let me try.'

He fed in the Plastix, the Radball chittered and ticked for a long time. Then the little armoured-glass panel lit up. A string of numbers and symbols jumbled behind it. They sorted themselves out, steadied, and spelled out EFFECTIVE.

Noll and Niven started cheering. The settlement invaded their goldfish bowls and they heard cheering at that end too: then Bang-Bang's voice saying, 'Well done.'

'Bet it hurt him to say that,' Noll muttered.

Banna came in. He said, 'Very good, very good! We are all very excited, you can hear ... Is the Radball still displaying EFFECTIVE?'

Niven went to look. The sign was flickering. It said EFFECTIVE ... then DELAY ... then EFFECTIVE ... then DELAY. At last it made up its mind and said DELAY 6 HRS. Noll and Niven reported this.

Banna said, 'Oh dear. That is not good. But it is not too bad either.'

'What does it mean, "Delay 6 hours"?' Noll asked.

'It has accepted the recode,' Banna's voice explained. 'But it has to Comm Earthside by radio for additional authority. It has to draw breath, so to speak. But six hours is a long time ... a pity. But only a pity.'

'So there's nothing more we can do?'

'No. Just come back carefully. Be very careful. Ride carefully!'

Bang-Bang's voice said, 'I endorse that. Get back in one piece. Over and out.' There was silence in their goldfish bowls.

They stood silent for a minute, getting used to the silence in their heads. They stared at the Radball and the dirty pit where the petrol had burned. As they watched, the Radball went *veeeeep* and closed the door of its hatch.

'Clever old you,' said Noll.

They checked over the Wheelie. She had a full tank of petrol, another few litres of spare fuel in two cans and she had used very little oil.

They tossed for who would take her first. Niven won. He straddled her, kicked her and she started first time. 'We'll change over every hour on the way back!' Niven said. 'After all, we're in no hurry!' He let in the clutch and the Wheelie snaked away over the ice. BA-RRRANG.

'Fifty-three miles,' Niven announced an hour later. He got off reluctantly. They stretched their legs.

Noll opened the petrol-filler and looked in the tank. 'Lots left,' he said. 'My go now.' He went through the gears fast, with plenty of throttle between each one. She loved it. Her rear tyre snaked, but the extra throttle seemed to make her dig in. 'There's a knack to it!' Noll shouted and swung Wheelie into a great circle in third. 'The more you give her, the better she sticks!' he said. Wheelie trembled with pleasure and the needle on the speedometer crept up.

Another hour, another change. They ignored the bleeps in their helmets – they could use them to home on the settlement at any time. Right now, Wheelie did the steering, picking out ridges and slopes and broken surfaces; anything but the flat monotony of the clear ground.

'Green weed!' Niven shouted. There was a big flat clump of the plant they had seen before to their left. Noll pointed Wheelie at the seaweedy stuff and charged it, whooping.

Wheelie went through it without feeling it. As he ripped her wheels through the weed, Noll kicked at it. Bits of fleshy weed flew through the air. Wheelie left a flattened track of grey-green pulp. They crossed and recrossed this track, cutting patterns in the weed and kicking out with their feet. Then, both yelling and singing, they left the weed behind and zoomed off in third, revs mounting.

They reached a sheet of flat, icy ground. They were still accelerating in third when everything went wrong. Noll braked and felt a sickening nothingness through the handlebars as the front wheel went. He throttled back and the rear wheel lost it too. Some instinct told Noll to steer into the slide: Wheelie skidded on endlessly, held upright by the soles of Noll's and Niven's boots. Then she hit rougher ice and somehow twitched herself upright. Noll held on to her, she slowed, they stopped. Wheelie burbled to herself. Noll and Niven sat completely still for a minute and more.

Niven said, 'Yes. Well. Time we changed over again.'

Noll made no reply. He checked Wheelie. Then he said, 'There's ice on this footrest, we only just missed going right over –'

'Well, we did miss it, so what the heck. What are you doing now?'

Noll said, 'Look. This splatty sole. I gashed it when we were making the fire and now it's opened right up. All that footwork when we were skidding ...' He showed Niven the sole. Niven said, 'That's dangerous. I'll get a MendPak. If that opens up just one little bit more, your suit is going to be full of Terramare 3 atmosphere. Which is bad for you.' He got a screwdriver from Wheelie's tool kit and started scraping away at the green weed in the crack. It was liquid ooze. Suddenly he stopped scraping and said, 'What the devil – !'

'Well, what?' said Noll.

Niven said nothing and scraped away, faster. Then he held up the screwdriver for Noll to see. The top was covered in grey-green slime – and with something else: the felt-like fibres with which the soles of an Ecosuit are made.

'The weed,' Niven said. 'It's eating away the sole! And it hasn't got far to go!' He dug at the soles of his own boots. Green slime and felt came away. He dropped the screwdriver and said, 'We're in trouble.'

'For God's sake!' Noll shouted. 'Another millimetre, and this crack will open right up! And then what?'

'Petrol,' Niven said. 'That might kill the weed. Let's try.' He ran to Wheelie, opened the filler cap of

79

the tank, got an oily rag from the tool kit and dipped it in petrol. He rubbed Noll's sole with the rag. The ooze shrank back, then closed in again.

'The stuff's alive!' Niven said.

He soaked the rag in petrol and bound it round Noll's foot so that the rag filled the crack. Noll was shaking. He said, 'And now what? How long will that hold out?'

'I don't know, how can I possibly know? All I know is – we must get back to the settlement. And quick. Get on the back, I'll drive.'

He kicked the starter and prayed: Wheelie heard. She started first time. Niven got the bleeps right and set course by them. He drove at a steady forty, going faster only when the ice ahead showed the satin sand sheen he knew to be safest.

'How far have we to go?' Noll said. His voice sounded small and clenched.

'Ask the settlement,' Niven replied. 'I'm concentrating on the bleeps. Don't want to waste even an inch.'

'They say sixty-three miles!' Noll said a minute later. 'When I think of all the time we wasted messing about –'

'Never mind that. Reach for one of the spare petrol cans. Open it and pour some of the petrol over the rag. I'll slow down!'

'Done,' said Noll. 'I'm screwing up the can. Speed up again.'

'Look at the tops of your boots and your legs,' Niven said. 'Anything wrong there? Is the weed attacking the rest of your suit or is it only the soles?'

'I can't see anything. Wait a minute! There's splat all over my legs – yours too – from when we were

80

kicking the plants ... The fabric seems softer there, it doesn't feel the same, it's sort of soft when you squeeze it – '

Niven said, 'That's all we need,' and let Wheelie show sixty on her speedometer. Then seventy. Then eighty.

When they came off, they were doing only thirty. The ground had rippling steps of ice in it, cracks like frozen waves. Wheelie rode them easily. But Niven, concentrating on the bleeps, did not see a step of ice that gently curved until it was almost in the direction of their travel. Wheelie's front tyre followed the curve – locked in it – and they were off, with Wheelie slithering along on her side bellowing and Noll and Niven rolling and sliding in a tangle of arms and legs.

They ran to Wheelie. Her engine was running and her rear wheel spinning, the spokes glittering. 'Thank heaven for that!' Niven said.

'But not for this,' Noll said – and pointed at the petrol tank. Petrol was still dribbling from the open tank. It made a patch that reached almost to the filler cap which lay clean and bright and innocent on the ice.

'Didn't put it on properly,' Niven muttered. 'Didn't secure it after I dipped the rag in for your foot. Sorry.'

Noll said, 'Yeah,' hopelessly. 'Well, might as well bolt the stable door now the horsepower's gone.' They put on the filler cap and, struggling, got Wheelie upright and on her stand. Then they took off the cap again and looked inside the tank.

'There's still some there. And we've got the reserve cans,' Niven said.

'Only one. And only a litre.'

'Oh. Well, let's fill up her tank and move on.'

'Yup.'

They tipped in the litre of petrol. There wasn't much petrol in the tank. They had sixty miles to go.

They started Wheelie. Niven drove. Her handlebars were crooked and a footrest was bent up. She had fallen on her throttlegrip side but the grip still twisted, a bit stiffly.

Niven's voice sounded in Noll's goldfish bowl: 'Are you getting bleeps?'

'Yes. Why? Aren't you?'

'No. I gave the old bowl a crack when we came off. I'm getting nothing, only you. Now what do we do?'

'You drive,' Noll said, 'I'll say "left" and "right". O.K.?'

'We'll try it,' Niven said.

It didn't work. You can tune yourself in to bleeps – make continuous, small corrections according to the notes and rhythms. You set up a flow of tiny movements. It doesn't work with spoken words. 'I'm stopping,' Niven said. 'We've got to think. Work something out.'

Noll said, 'Look, I'll drive. We haven't got far to go.'

'You can't. You've got to keep that foot still, you can't push pedals and things, you'll open the crack up. If it really opens, you're finished.'

'I'll try. We're not getting on fast enough. We're zigzagging. Move over.'

Noll got off, inspected the cracked sole, saw the ooze creeping over the petrol-soaked rag, getting used to the evaporating petrol, pushing it aside. The felt-like fibres were softening and becoming like the grey-green ooze.

He said nothing, engaged first, and concentrated on the bleeps: there was nothing else he wanted to think about. Second, third, fourth ... Wheelie roared on over the endless ice-locked sand of Terramare 3.

Niven said, 'Know what? We're going to make it.'

As he spoke, Noll yelled, and braked. They slid to a halt.

Noll leapt off Wheelie and said, 'MendPack, quick. The crack's opened right up!'

Steam vented from Noll's Ecosuit as the ice-cold, poisonous atmosphere began its invasion. 'I'm cold ... cold ...'

'Put your foot up!' Niven began packing MendPak strips into the oozing gap in Noll's sole. The gap was too jelly-like, too wet. It had no proper shape.

Noll moaned, 'I'm cold. Cold!'

Niven could hear his teeth chattering. He said, 'Can you breathe?'

Noll said, 'I don't know ... There's a taste of something and I'm cold –'

Niven said, 'Are you turned right up? Have you got the heat full on? Have you?'

Noll said, 'I don't know, it's cold ... No, I haven't. Now I have. But it's still cold ...'

Niven said, 'Get back on Wheelie. Quick. Get on. And hold on tight. Are you holding on? Tell me when you're ready, we're going. Fast.'

Noll said, 'It's cold. My foot's cold. I'm cold all over –'

'Hold tight. Really tight. Now!'

Wheelie's rear tyre dug in and they were off. Niven felt panic tightening in his throat. He let the needle creep up, through the sixties, through the seventies. And then, above the roar of the engine, he heard the bleeps. His goldfish bowl had mended itself. Luck! Perhaps old Wheelie's vibrations had jiggled the connections together. For an instant, his panic died down. But then Noll began raving. 'Oh, well,' Niven told himself, 'as long as he can talk he's alive ...'

He felt a heavy weight fall on his neck: Noll's head. Niven shouted: 'Noll! Noll! You with me?'

'What? My nose hurts. And my throat. What?'

'Noll, put your arms round me! Hang on to me!'

'I can't do that. I can't breathe. I'm cold. Aren't you cold?'

All the same, Niven felt Noll's arms settle loosely round his waist. He said, 'Hang on, Noll! Come on, grip me!' The arms tightened a little. Noll began to mumble about cold, and a sore throat. Niven gave Wheelie a thousandth of an inch more throttle. She was going so fast now that even keeping her on the bleeps took all Niven's courage. She was flying on ice, there was no feel from the ground at all.

The settlement came in, they were trying to tell him something. He yelled, 'Get off, get off! I can't hear the bleeps!'

Noll began to talk and wouldn't stop. 'Meet you in the Centre,' he said, 'It's cold in here. Warm in the Centre. This stuff tastes splatty, they shouldn't serve stuff like this ...' His voice was weak and hoarse. He started coughing. His cough sounded like a polite little girl's – 'Ah-hoo! Ah-hoo! Hoo, hoo, hoo!' He wouldn't stop. It got in the way of the bleeps, Niven couldn't hear the bleeps –

The settlement! There was its mast and a glint of a man-made shape, a straight hard line. Buildings! His hand twitched on the throttle, wanting to give it still more – but Niven stopped himself, there was no grip left in either wheel and the iced sand was slick. Was it really the settlement? The bleeps suddenly changed to a constant beeeep and he knew it was. Home and dry.

One of Noll's arms fell away from his waist and he felt the sickening shift of balance as Noll's whole body slumped. The Wheelie tried to plough away to the left, he let her do it because if Noll fell off –

He could not brake, he let the Wheelie find any course that would keep them upright. He saw a slur of red beneath the grey ice, that meant sand on or near the surface, perhaps he might risk braking ... he feathered on the brakes so lightly that he didn't know if the linings were even touching the drums. Then a bit more, a little bit more – Wheelie slowed, she really did slow, he was sure of it. But Noll was slipping sideways –

He shouted, 'To hell with it!' and braked, not hard but definitely: and Wheelie slowly came to a stop: and Noll slid sideways, very gently and fell on the ice, with helmet bouncing: and Niven's ears were full of voices from the settlement.

He yelled. 'Shut up! Shut up!' and got Wheelie on her stand. Then he tried to get Noll up but he was heavy and his Ecosuit was slippery. He got him half-way up but then he slipped and his helmet hit the ground again, a wicked thud.

Noll's eyes opened and he said, 'I'm not well, I'm cold ...' and he started coughing again.

Niven said, 'You've got to help me get you up. You've got to get up. UP!' He got Noll half up and half down, then realized he didn't know what to do with him. The settlement was still talking, but how could they help? He shouted, 'Shut up!' again and pushed Noll towards Wheelie.

Noll coughed and said, 'This stuff in my throat, it's poison ...'

Niven saw what he must do. Without pushing the Wheelie over, he had to get Noll on to it, on to the front seat. But Noll was coming alive again, he was struggling and coughing and saying, 'Don't touch me! You're cold, you're like ice! Don't touch me!'

Niven said, 'Look, Noll! There's the Wheelie! We're going to ride her! The Wheelie, Noll, the Wheelie!'

Noll said, 'Where?' and fell on his hands and knees.

Niven got him up and with a last despairing effort, almost threw him face-down over the back wheel of the motorbike. Noll's helmet slammed down on the headlamp. Niven grunted 'Good' – straddled the bike – and pushed Noll forward until he lay with his head between the headlamp and the crook of the handlebar and his chest along the petrol tank. His feet touched the ground. Niven kicked his legs aside, got his feet to the pedals, engaged first, let the clutch in.

Wheelie didn't move!

Niven sobbed, cursed and gave her more throttle. Still she didn't move! Clutch gone. And then Niven realized that Wheelie was still on her stand, the rear wheel was just spinning around doing nothing –

He rocked the dead weight of Wheelie over her stand, shouted, 'He'll be dead in a few minutes! Open the doors!' – and let in the clutch. Wheelie staggered away, lurching left and right and all over the place under Noll's weight on the front wheel. Niven got second gear, accelerated and she steadied but it was like steering a lead pig through porridge. He was going away from the settlement! He pulled the pig round, twisted the handgrip and let her go. She was better at speed.

Excited voices in his head were telling him to do this and do that and Noll's feet were trailing in the ice. Was Noll alive? His goldfish bowl jiggled and bumped lifelessly, there were no sounds from him. Even the coughing had stopped.

Third gear. More speed to keep her steady. Then the big doors of the settlement swung aside and the black hole behind them lit up and grew bigger and bigger as Wheelie rushed towards them. Niven found that he was cold, very cold. It surprised him, the Eco-suits never let you down. There was a taste in his mouth, a splatty taste, his chest hurt too. He thought he saw people, and Su, and a wall with BAY 5 written on it. The people all had their mouths open and there was a noise like the sea in his helmet. Cheering? Then the wall came at him like a wave and hit him and everything spun round and crashed. The crash went on and on, repeating itself sickeningly but farther away from Niven. That would be the Wheelie, plunging on, riderless ... Yet the sound like the sea, or cheering, or whatever it was, still continued. And he really did see Su, she was floating above him. Her hands came down and pulled at his helmet. He felt other hands. He said, 'Ah. I'm lying down and they're standing up–'

They got the helmet off and Su was shouting at him. She shouted, 'Move your arms! Move your legs! Come on, Niven! Do it!' So he did it, to oblige her. He even sat up and glimpsed Noll, who was wagging his head.

And then the sound of the sea, the cheering noise, started again and everyone was smiling and Su gave him a kiss. He said to her, 'Look, I'm cold, cold, they don't understand ...'

The faces turned a strange bleached colour and started to spin. He had dreams, long dreams. He wasn't sure they were true or false. Wheelie leaking petrol from her handlebars ... Bang-Bang eating a plateful of the grey-green plants and saying, 'What does he mean, cold? They're hot, hot, piping hot!' ... Su on the Wheelie, saying, 'I'll just drive her down the elephant's trunk. Easy!' Niven tried to stop her, but she drove off, faster and faster along the elephant's trunk – there was a chink of light at the end of it, it was coming closer, there'd be a crash!

Then there was light, light everywhere. He inspected it through half-closed eyes, not trusting it. A dream? He opened his eyes gradually. Not a dream: he was in a bed, a MedSec bed, and the mummied figure lying beside him on the other bed was Noll, covered in bandages.

A day later Niven was on his feet and hobbling about the settlement. Everywhere, people smiled and made jokes and patted his back. But Noll could not get up. He was covered in frostbite and bandages. So he heard the news from Niven, grumbled, then played endless games of draughts and solitaire on a tiny Sportacom, losing all the time. 'When's Su coming?' he said.

She came, and Noll cheered up. He said, 'We're going to get medals. Isn't that right, Su? Big flashy heroes' medals?'

Su said, 'Everyone on the settlement wants you to get the biggest, shiniest medals going!'

Niven said, 'Everyone? What about Bang-Bang?'

Su's smile faded.

Noll said, 'What's the Wheelie really like, Niven? How badly damaged?'

'I keep telling you,' Niven said, 'she'll be all right. She slid along bumping herself. She's just got bent bars, a lever spoiled, footrest twisted, that sort of thing –'

'What about the petrol tank?'

Su laughed. 'You and that petrol tank! You're like a mother hen with a prize egg! The petrol tank is *all right*, not a *scratch*, not a *dent* –'

'Well, I hope you're right ... We couldn't replace the transfers. Not ever. You know, the emblem –'

Two grinning faces appeared round the edge of the door: a Mech and a Tech. 'You've got a visitor this afternoon! Very big-deal visitor!'

'Medal time,' Niven said grandly. 'We're so brave. Is that what you mean?'

The two faces looked serious and one said, 'Look, everyone's on your side. We'll make sure you get what you deserve –'

There were footsteps, and the two faces disappeared. 'What was that about?' Niven asked Su. 'What did they mean about "getting what we deserve" –'

Su said, 'Bang-Bang's coming to see you in person. With medals, or something.'

'"Or something"?' Noll said. 'You don't sound very cheerful about it, Su.'

'Well, he's coming this afternoon. And I might come in too. Come in strong. Wait and see.'

Bang-Bang came and gave them their medals: a Galactic Star 2nd Class each. You get the Galactic Star 2nd Class for anything from turning up for duty to cleaning your teeth up and down instead of sideways. It is not a top award. Noll and Niven took their medals in silence.

'So much for the pleasant part of my duty,' Bang-Bang said. 'Now for the unpleasant part.' When he said this, his voice sounded more cheerful. 'In performing the praiseworthy deed for which you earned these medals, you committed certain crimes and admitted to several more. I need not enumerate them, but I must deal with them. I have already dealt with Mr Banna –'

Su came in with chin stuck out and frightened eyes. She held a little Comm set in her hand. She said, 'I was involved, sir. May I stay?'

Bang-Bang glanced uneasily at the PortaComm and did not answer her. 'I have already dealt with Mr Banna,' he repeated.

But Su interrupted. 'How, sir?' she asked.

'By demotion. And I intend to issue instructions concerning his pension.'

'Ah,' said Su, and drew a deep breath before she said, 'I wouldn't do that, sir. I'd leave him alone. I'd leave *everything* alone.'

Bang-Bang gaped, glared – and roared. But Su, her voice metallic with fear and determination, said, 'Beg to report, sir, there's a skeleton in your cupboard. So before you deal with Mr Banna – and these two – and me – hadn't you better deal with your own skeleton?'

'I don't think you understand what you are letting yourself in for, young lady,' Bang-Bang said in a low voice.

'I was thinking just the same thing about you, sir,' Su said. Her voice trembled but her eyes were steady. 'The settlement likes Noll and Niven, sir. There's a lot of support for them. And as I say, there's this skeleton. Would you like to hear it speak?' The little machine in her hand lit up and displayed a group of letters and numbers: BRDCO/4.

'That's just a RadRec designation, sir,' Su explained. 'Not interesting. And this one – COMM TM3 – that just means "Appointed to the command of Terramare 3". That's more interesting. That was *you*, sir, thirteen years ago.'

More groups of letters and figures. 'And here comes the bull, sir!' Su said, almost cheerfully. 'This group means, "In accordance with the Regulations laid down and hereby repeated" ... and here come all those Regulations ... and here's your acknowledgement and Declaration to Obey. But you didn't obey the Regulations, did you sir? You didn't site the settlement in the place designated by your geologists. And when you had to move the settlement, you didn't move the Radball, did you, sir?'

'There was a war,' Bang-Bang said. 'You stupid child, I had more important work to do. More important than some absurd little settlement, an outpost of the galaxy –'

Banna's voice sounded in the PortaComm. 'And you went off to the war, didn't you?' It crackled. 'And won some real medals ... And when a junior officer replaced you here, you sent him a Confidential instructing him to cover up for you about the Radball, isn't that right? You said, "Don't move the Radball, because that means a recode and a report and we'll both be in trouble." That's more or less what you said, isn't it, sir? With a little blackmail, and a few promises you never kept?'

'There was a war,' Bang-Bang said hollowly.

In the PortaComm, Banna's voice shook with fury. 'A war, a glorious war!' it said. 'And you did well in it! And you fiddled the RadRec. You entered a false record. You even tried to delete the true record, but you didn't. You couldn't. And now I've got it!'

The Commanding Officer opened his mouth, but no words came out at first. When he could speak, he said, 'Very well. You want something. What is it?'

Su said, 'He wants justice.'

Banna's voice said, 'Yes, justice. You leave the boys alone! They're not going to be Cargohumpers all their lives! And leave the girl alone, she's –'

'It's Mr Banna that matters,' Noll said.

Niven said, 'Look, you're an officer and a gentleman and all that. Let's do a gentlemanly deal, like the one you did about the Radball all those years ago. We keep Wheelie, and Banna keeps pension and rank –'

'And you keep your mouth shut,' Noll said, staring hard at Bang-Bang. 'Agreed?'

The Galaxy is a big place. Light-years big. From the planet Earth, you can see many of the planets that form it; and imagine the vast, invisible web of power that links it, powers its tools and spacecraft, serves its works and peoples and purposes.

In only one small outpost of the Galaxy is there an exception to the rule of Rad. The exception has to be coaxed and kicked, tickled with feeler gauges and oily fingers, fed with smelly and forbidden fluids. When all this and much more is done, the weird old relic of a cruder age goes BA-RRRANG, emits a little smoke and moves bits of itself up or down, round and round, to and fro: and people nod their heads at each other, smiling.

It's all strictly illegal. But it's still going on in Terramare 3.

About the Author

Nicholas Fisk wrote his first complete book when he was nine. It was about a baby fox and was very sentimental. He first earned money from writing when he was sixteen. When he finished his R A F service he became an actor, jazz musician, illustrator and writer for all kinds of publications.

His interests include snorkelling, cars, old microscopes, building a swimming pool, photography (he has published a book on the subject), and a dozen other things. He finds that writing is hard and lonely work, but enjoys writing 'science fiction' (meaning stories about extraordinary things that *could* happen) for young people. They seem to understand how fast the world is changing, whereas most older people do not.

Other Puffins by Nicholas Fisk

SPACE HOSTAGES

Some children investigate a spaceship that lands on the local cricket pitch, and find themselves kidnapped by the man inside it. Then they discover that he is dying and have to find out how to work the ship.

TRILLIONS

When a heavy shower of Trillions fell on Harbourtown, newspaper headlines began to look like science fiction. What was their purpose – friend or foe?

GRINNY

Why couldn't Great Aunt Emma remember anything about Granny, who was supposed to be her sister, and why was she so scared of electricity, as if she thought it could leak? And why, on that horrifying night when Tim and Beth went to her bedroom, was she shining in the dark and lying like an Egyptian mummy with her eyes wide open, staring at nothing, but still grinning?

TIME TRAP

Dano was a hopeful, a Teen, with a skimmer that could do 100 mph and all the sports gear in the Catalogue, but it wasn't enough. He wanted to get out of Homebody Unit 326 and be responsible for his own life.

ANTIGRAV

The tiny island seemed an ideal place for scientists from all round the world to meet and relax. But on the beach lay a small red pebble which had remarkable powers, and soon three children who had gone along for a holiday found themselves trying to keep the pebble out of enemy hands.

A RAG, A BONE AND A HANK OF HAIR

After a terrible nuclear accident the birthrate has dropped dramatically. The only hope appears to lie with the Reborns – new people made chemically by scientists. But the Reborns have been given free will and no one is quite certain how they will behave ...

Heard about the Puffin Club?

... it's a way of finding out more about Puffin books and authors, of winning prizes (in competitions), sharing jokes, a secret code, and perhaps seeing your name in print! When you join you get a copy of our magazine, *Puffin Post*, sent to you four times a year, a badge and a membership book.

For details of subscription and an application form, send a stamped addressed envelope to:

The Puffin Club Dept A
Penguin Books Limited
Bath Road
Harmondsworth
Middlesex UB7 0DA

and if you live in Australia, please write to:

The Australian Puffin Club
Penguin Books Australia Limited
P.O. Box 257
Ringwood
Victoria 3134